HELL OF A CHRISTMAS

ABBI GLINES

NEW YORK TIMES BESTSELLING AUTHOR

Hell of a Christmas
The Mississippi Smoke Series
Copyright © 2025 by Abbi Glines
All rights reserved.
Visit my website at https://abbiglinesbooks.com

Cover Designer: Sarah Sentz, Enchanting Romance Designs
www.enchantingromancedesigns.com
Editor: Jovana Shirley, Unforeseen Editing
www.unforeseenediting.com
Formatting: Melissa Stevens, The Illustrated Author
www.theillustratedauthor.com

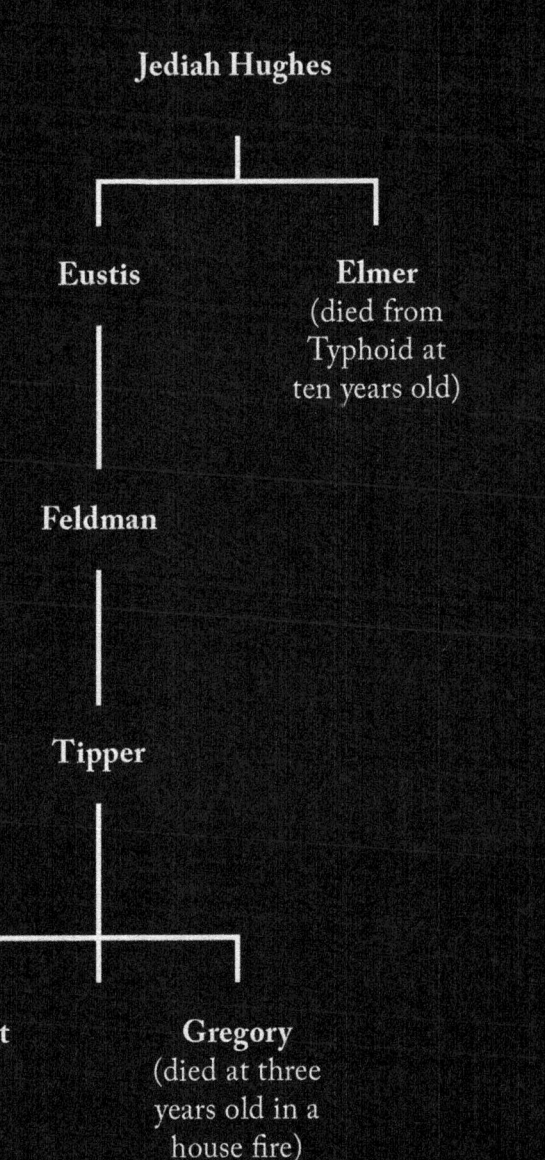

• THE FAMILY •
started by Jediah Hughes. It began with horse racing, moonshine, and illegal arms in the early 1900s

Jediah Hughes

Eustis

Elmer
(died from
Typhoid at
ten years old)

Feldman

Tipper

Garrett

Gregory
(died at three
years old in a
house fire)

• THE HUGHES •
Hughes Farm

Garrett Hughes (BOSS in books 1-9)
Wife: **Fawn Parker Hughes** → *SCORCH*

Blaise Hughes (Current BOSS/oldest son)
Wife: **Madeline Walsh Hughes** (parents Etta Marks/dead and Liam

Trev Hughes
Fiancée: **Gypsi Parker** (also stepsister) → *FIRECRACKER*

Cree Elias Hughes → *SMOKESHOW* and *FIREBALL*

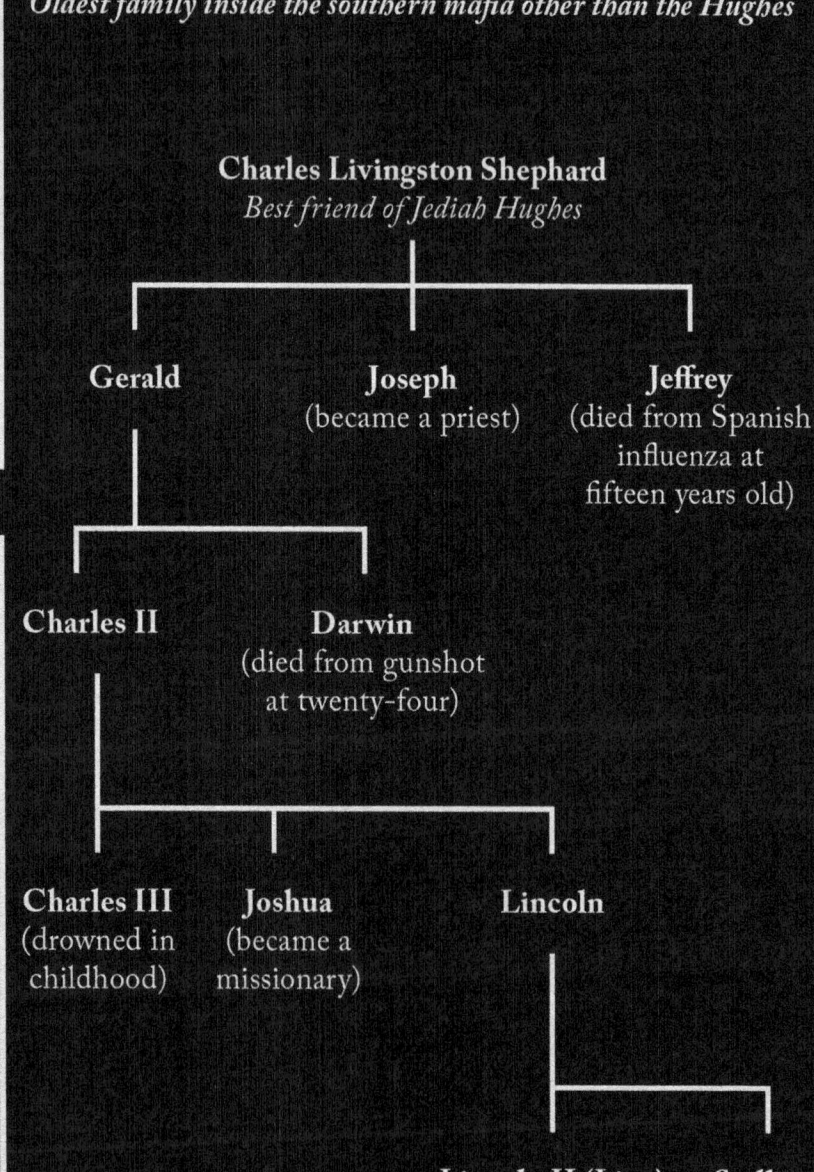

• THE SHEPHARDS •
Oldest family inside the southern mafia other than the Hughes

Charles Livingston Shephard
Best friend of Jediah Hughes

Gerald

Joseph
(became a priest)

Jeffrey
(died from Spanish influenza at fifteen years old)

Charles II

Darwin
(died from gunshot at twenty-four)

Charles III
(drowned in childhood)

Joshua
(became a missionary)

Lincoln

Lincoln II (Linc)

Stellan

Mississippi Branch

Linc Shephard
(left Florida to run Mississippi Branch when **Levi** was twenty-two)

Florida Branch

Levi Shephard
Wife: **Aspen Chance Shephard** → *WHISKEY SMOKE*

Georgia Branch
Shephard Ranch

Stellan Shephard
Wife: **Mandilyn Shephard**

Thatcher
→ *DEMONS*

Sebastian
→ *SMOLDER*

• THE KINGSTONS •
Mars Kingston joined the family in 1921

Mars Kingston
Childhood friend of Jediah Hughes

Hollis

Son
(died in childhood)

Atticus

Son
(died in childhood)

Rollin

Raul

Creed

Barrett

Florida Branch

Creed Kingston (dead)
Wife: **Abigail Kingston** (dead)

Huck
Wife: **Trinity Bennett Kingston**
→ *SMOKE BOMB*

Hayes (dead)
engaged to **Trinity**
at his death

Georgia Branch

Barrett Kingston
Wife: **Annette Kingston**

Storm
→ *SIZZLING*
and *STORM*

Lela
*Book coming in
2025*

Nailyah
*Book coming in
2025*

• THE HOUSTONS •
Joined the family through horse racing in 1938

Kenneth Houston Wife: **Melanie Houston**

|

Saxon Houston
Wife: **Haisley Slate Houston** →
SMOKIN' HOT

|

Winter Noel Houston

• THE LEVINES •
Joined the family in 1977

Alister Levine

|

Mississippi Branch

Luther Levine
Ex-Wife: **Chloe Wall**
(Moved from Florida when **Kye** was nineteen)

|

Florida Branch

Kye Levine
Wife: **Genesis Stoll Levine** → *BURN*

|

Jagger Henley Levine

• THE PRESLEYS •
Joined the family after graduation

Gage Presley
Best friend of Blaise Hughes in high school
Wife: **Shiloh Carmichael Presley** → *STRAIGHT FIRE*

· THE SALAZARS ·
Joined the family through horse racing in 1958

Georgia Branch only

Efrain Salazar

Gabriel Salazar (dead)
Wife: **Maeme Salazar**

Ronan Salazar
Wife: **Jupiter Salazar**

Birdie

King Salazar
→ *SLAY* and
SLAY KING
Mother: **Estela Salazar**

• THE JONES •
Joined the family through joined real-estate in 1966

Georgia Branch only

Hoyt Jones

Monte
Fiancée: **Bay Mintley**

Roland
Wife: **Luella Jones**

Wilder Jones
Wife: **Oakley Watson
Jones** →*ASHES*

Wells Jones
*Book date
coming soon*

Teller Jones
*Book coming
in 2025*

Sarah Jones

• THE RICES •

Oldest family in Missisippi Branch. Hiram Rice left Ocala in 1912 to move to Madison, Mississippi and run a speakeasies in Jackson and one on Madison both Jediah Hughes had purchased. Illegal gambling as well as moonshine was sold inside the bars.

Mississippi Branch

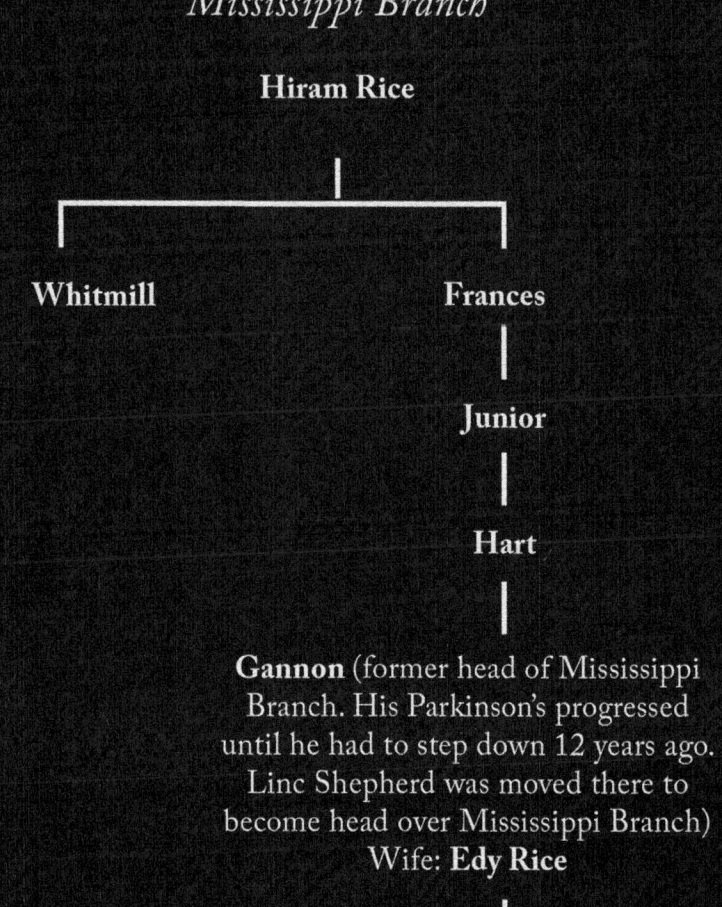

Hiram Rice

Whitmill   **Frances**

Junior

Hart

Gannon (former head of Mississippi Branch. His Parkinson's progressed until he had to step down 12 years ago. Linc Shepherd was moved there to become head over Mississippi Branch)
Wife: **Edy Rice**

Fia Rice Castron   **Saylor**
(married to a member
of Louisiana Branch)

• THE CARVERS •

Awbrey Carver joined the family in 1928 through bootlegging and running illegal gambling rings.

Mississippi Branch only

Awbrey Carver

Robert

Hale
Wife: **Lethia Carver** (dead)

Ransom   **Opal**   **Than**

• THE CASHES •
The Cash Ranch

Mississippi Branch only

Hawkins Cash
Joined the family in 1922 through horse racing

Samuel
(shot and killed at
20 years old)

William

Fender
Wife: **Grissele Cash**

Bane
→ *TORE UP*

Crosby

• THE SAVELLES •
Savelle Stables

Mississippi Branch

Oz Savelle
joined the Family in 1967 through horse

Jonas
Wife: **Ellender Savelle**

Oz   Forge   Kash

Alabama Branch

Kash Savelle
moved to Alabama Branch when he turned 21

• THE BOWENS •
Lewis Bowen joined the family in 1975

Mississippi Branch
Lewis Bowen
Oz Savelle's best friend since childhood

Malbrough 'Mal'
Ex-Wife: **Celeste**

Locke   **Gathe**

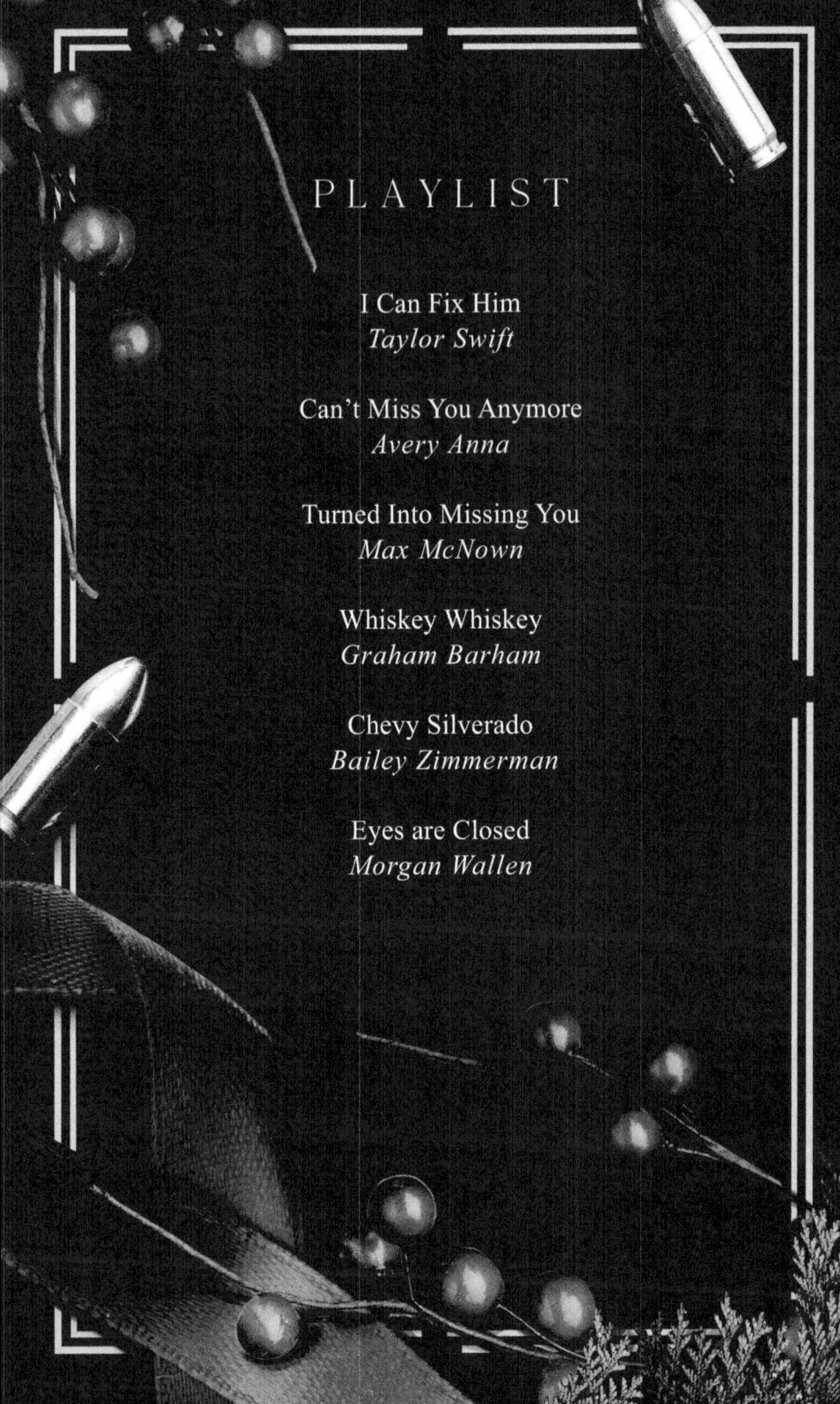

PLAYLIST

I Can Fix Him
Taylor Swift

Can't Miss You Anymore
Avery Anna

Turned Into Missing You
Max McNown

Whiskey Whiskey
Graham Barham

Chevy Silverado
Bailey Zimmerman

Eyes are Closed
Morgan Wallen

Carolina
Blake Whitten

The Baby
Blake Shelton

Sun to Me
Zach Bryan

ACKNOWLEDGMENTS

Happy Holidays and Happy New Year!

I hope you enjoyed Kash Savelle's story. He was always the one Mississippi boy we knew very little about. You'll see more of Kash and Cressida in UP TO NO GOOD coming next month. While the Savelle's start the new year facing their mother's sickness, Forge finds comfort in an unexpected place.

To those who make it happen every single time:

Britt is always the first I mention because without him, our house might literally fall apart.

Emerson for surviving without me. I would say she didn't complain but that would be a lie. There is always a lot of standing at my office door and scowling at me.

My older children, who live in other states, they called and texted and were also ignored. I felt bad but I replied "Writing, deadline, will call when finished." And they didn't mind but they also didn't stop calling and texting so... anyway. Thankfully my second granddaughter has waited until after I finished the edits on this one before making her appearance. I am ready for her now. She can hurry it on along. God, knows her momma is ready too.

My editor, Jovana Shirley at Unforeseen Editing. She worked with my tight schedule, and I would be screwed without her. She's a God send. (this seems to be happening monthly so I might as well copy and paste this with each Acknowledgments section) I need to start sending her wine baskets every month for putting up with me.

My formatter, Melissa Stevens at The Illustrated Author. Who has never let me down. She always does a speedy turn around for me (monthly I might add). She makes my books beautiful inside. Her work is the best formatting I've ever had in my books. She works with my tight schedule, the deadlines I miss and always makes sure I have an excellent finished product.

Autumn Gantz, at Wordsmith Publicity, for saving me from losing my mind and taking over all the things that I can't keep up with anymore. Her help allows me to write this quickly. She reminds me of the things I need to do. I don't think I would have been able to keep up with this one book a month schedule without her.

Beta readers, who come through every time: Jerilyn Martinez, and Vicci Kaighan. I love y'all!

Sarah Sentz, Enchanting Romance Designs, for my book cover. Again, she nailed it. I have no visual creativity to give her any help in the matter. But she manages to create something I adore every time.

Abbi's Army, for being my support and cheering me on. I love y'all!

My readers, for allowing me to write books. Without you, this wouldn't be possible.

Here is to a NEW YEAR with more Mississippi Mafia books and the first dip into the Louisiana Branch.

To every maker of magic during the holiday season.

PROLOGUE

CRESSIDA

Sixteen Years Old

Was there a blue that could describe his eyes accurately? I didn't think so, and God knew I'd lain in bed trying to think of one since Kash Savelle had locked them on me the first day of school. The clearest sky on a summer day, the color of a perfect raindrop, the ocean in the South Pacific perhaps might come close.

Holding my laptop tightly to my chest, I scanned the crowded hallway as those around me talked about the football game on Friday night. Our team had beaten the other one by over twenty points. Kash had run in two touchdowns. Calloway Short dropped her pom-poms and took off running to him when the game was over. I didn't stay around to watch the rest of that. Instead, I went home and did my best to shove the image of the head cheerleader slash prom queen slash pain in my ass throwing herself into his arms out of my mind. But getting Kash Savelle out of my head had been impossible. He had seared his image into my brain with those damn eyes and that cocky grin of his.

I wasn't doing much to fight this attraction to him either. Like, at the moment, when I should be hurrying to my first period class and going over the questions for our quiz, I was instead looking for him. Wanting a glimpse. Oh, who was I kidding? I wanted to see if he noticed me, smiled at me, spoke to me. I had thought of little else all weekend.

"Tell me who you're looking for so intently, and I'll help you find them." The thick Southern drawl was one I would recognize anywhere. It was the only voice that had ever sent a thrill through my body and caused instant goose bumps.

I spun around, drawing in a sharp breath as my heart took off in a wild flutter.

There he was. All six foot two of him, with his messy hair the color of ink and those eyes that made even the bluest sky appear lackluster. The corner of his mouth quirked as his eyes glinted with ... I wasn't sure, but it sent a shiver through me. Was it interest? Oh God, let it be interest.

"Kash! Where did y—" another male voice called out, then paused mid-sentence when Kash held up a hand and stopped whatever they were going to say, keeping his gaze on mine.

"I'm busy," he said, and then he winked at me.

I was going to melt. Right here on the floor. Become an instant puddle. Kash Savelle had winked at me.

"I see ... later then," the other guy replied, and Kash gave a small nod of his head in agreement.

"Now, who was it you need to find, beautiful?" he asked me.

Breathe, Cressida. Do not embarrass yourself. You have his attention. Make the most of it.

He called me beautiful!

"I was, um, just, uh ..." I stammered like an idiot. What did I say? That I'd been looking for him? Telling him that might scare him off. It gave stalker vibes. "No one." *Liar.*

He raised one eyebrow. "You sure about that? Because I stood behind you for a solid minute, and you were so locked in that you didn't notice you were being admired."

Admired? Me. He had been looking at me.

"Oh," I breathed, unable to say more than that with my heart racing.

A deep chuckle sent a bolt of pleasure through me. "Damn, you're sweet. Lucky for you I've got a conscience and I'm gonna walk away."

Wait, what? Walk away?

He reached out and took a lock of my hair, then twirled it around his finger before dropping it with a sigh.

"Why ... why are you walking away?" I blurted, desperate to keep him here.

His eyes seemed to twinkle with something, but whether it was amusement or not, I couldn't tell. There was a darkness there too. I'd seen it before. It felt a bit threatening, but then he'd smile, and it would vanish. All that was left was the clear blue.

"Because I don't break pretty things," he said before giving me one last look, then left me standing there, feeling as if he'd sucked every ounce of joy from my life.

3

ONE

CRESSIDA

Twenty-Three Years Old

"Order up," Harland Wilts, the only cook at the twenty-four-hour greasy-spoon diner I'd unfortunately been working at for the past month called out.

There were two truckers, a table of firemen who had just gotten off the night shift, and Burt—the homeless man I had given ten dollars to so he could come in and eat since the temperature had dropped this week.

I worked from four in the morning until four in the afternoon. The hours were long and exhausting, but if I ever wanted to save enough money to get a better place to live, then I needed to work the twelve-hour shifts. Truth was, I wasn't far from being as homeless as Burt. Seeing him buried under old blankets on my walk to work reminded me how close I was to being in that situation. It was still better than the alternative. Running had been my only option. No one was going to find me here. Even if my father tried, which I doubted he would, he wouldn't look for me at a place like the diner.

"You gonna let him sit there all day? I can smell him from here," Harland grumbled, looking toward Burt with disgust.

Harland was balding, with a large gut from beer and a poor diet. He was also as greasy as the food he fried. I didn't like him, but I had to work with him every day.

"You can't smell anything over the scent of fried meat," I replied, snatching up the early bird special that the trucker at table six had ordered.

What the special should be named was a *heart attack waiting to happen*. Four fried eggs, hash browns covered in cheese and bacon, two biscuits with sausage gravy, and cheese grits. If Maybelle and Tipper Elp—the couple who owned this place—decided to put calories on the menu, then they would likely go out of business. This one meal had to have at least five thousand calories in it.

"Sun's come up. He's got blankets. He needs to go," Harland told me.

If I replied the way I wanted to, then he'd be difficult to work with the rest of the day. I bit my tongue and walked away to deliver the plates of unhealthy food to the trucker instead. The high today was only going to be thirty-one. That was rare in Mississippi, even two days before December. I was not letting Burt stay out in that. He was almost seventy years old. Harland could go sit out in it though.

On Thanksgiving, we'd been packed with the usual clientele and some single dads with their kids. The cold snap had hit that day, but there were no available tables for Burt. I took him out a meal and a large box I'd saved from a recent delivery. It wasn't heat, but it had been something to help keep him out of the wind.

"Here you go," I said brightly as I set the plate down in front of the trucker. "I'll freshen up that cup of coffee," I assured him. "Can I get you anything else?"

I tried not to cringe at the leering smile he gave me. It came with the job. Most of the time, the customers didn't harass me.

"Could use a little hot sauce," he replied.

"I'll be right back." Not waiting around for him to say anything more and wanting to get away from him as he let his eyes wander down my body, I turned to go grab the coffeepot.

The sound of the bell from the door being opened caused me to pause. This was a seat-yourself establishment, but I needed to see where they'd be sitting and how many so I could grab them menus. What I expected to see was another trucker or perhaps one of the night-shift employees from the hospital less than a mile away. It wasn't either. It was a woman and she was out of place. The lady had to be lost. Maybe she was passing through town. It wasn't dangerous around here, but she wouldn't know that. I doubted she'd ever stepped foot in a place like this. I knew her purse was a Louis Vuitton, her heels were Louboutin, and I'd bet my next three tips that the Burberry scarf around her neck was one hundred percent authentic.

I decided to go see if I could help her before getting table six's coffee and hot sauce. The scent of her perfume greeted me as I reached her, and it smelled as expensive as she looked. She had to be from out of town. Sure, there was money in Madison, but they wouldn't be coming in this place for a meal.

"Good morning," I said as she watched me approach. "Can I help you?" I didn't add, *Because we both know you're not here for the food.*

She began tugging off her elbow-length butter-colored leather gloves and glanced around. "Yes, thank you," she replied. "I'd like a cup of coffee." Then she turned her gaze back to mine. "I'll take that booth if that's okay." She nodded toward one that sat farthest away from the rest of the customers.

"Uh, yes, um, all right."

I battled between just letting her sit down and getting her what she'd asked for or telling her how bad the coffee actually was. Harland made it so strong that it could make hair grow on your arms. Not to mention, it was some cheap brand that came in bulk. From the looks of this woman, I imagined she drank something more bougie. Like French-pressed from freshly ground beans.

The woman headed to the booth, and I watched her, wincing at the thought of her sitting down even though I'd wiped it clean an hour ago. She was most likely wearing Chanel under that coat. Or some other designer that cost more than what the owners of this place made in a year.

Finally turning back toward the coffeepot, I noticed some of the other diners staring over at her curiously. She seemed oblivious to the fact, or she just didn't care. I hurried to get the things for table six and then went to pour her what might be the worst coffee she had ever tasted. She was texting on her phone when I returned, but she stopped and lifted her gaze to meet mine.

"This is bad," I said under my breath so that Harland didn't hear me. "I just thought you should be warned before taking a sip."

Her lips quirked up in amusement. "I'll proceed with caution," she replied.

"I can get you real cream from the back if you like instead of the powder stuff they have for you to use on the table," I told her, nodding toward the condiment basket.

She glanced at it, then swung her eyes back to mine. "That would be more preferable," she replied. "Thank you."

7

Relieved to be able to do something to make the coffee taste possibly drinkable, I started to turn and go back to the kitchen.

"Before you go," she said, stopping me.

I looked back at her, hoping she wasn't going to order food. We had not one thing on our menu that she would want.

"Do you like working here?" she asked.

That caused me to pause. My hackles rose, and I took a step back. She didn't belong here. She was asking questions about *me*. Had my father sent her? Or worse ... had Arthur? I swallowed nervously. I was an adult. I hadn't thought they would find me here, but if so, they couldn't force me to come back. Besides, my stepmother had to be thrilled I'd left. She wouldn't want me to return. I would quit and find another job.

"Why are you asking me that?" The defensive edge in my tone was sharp, but she didn't wince.

"Because you seem out of place here."

I seemed out of place? Had she looked in a mirror?

A short laugh escaped me. "I was thinking the same about you."

She smiled then, a full one, as amusement danced in her eyes. "It's a first for me. But it seems I might have found more than bad coffee. You see, I'm in need of a sitter for my elderly aunt. She needs help around the house and someone to drive her places." Her gaze flickered across the restaurant with disdain before coming back to me. "I don't need to know why you're here, but I like your honesty and willingness to help. Your concern over my coffee and desire to make it better when you didn't have to try. It says a lot about your character. The job would pay better, and, well"—she paused—"Aunt Glenda is delightful company. You'd have to live there though. In one of the guest rooms. We don't want her to be alone at night."

I blinked. Processed what I had heard and tried not to stand there, gaping at her. She didn't know me, and she was offering me a job and to live for free with her elderly aunt?

I was sleeping on a blanket on the floor in a studio apartment in a very bad part of town. It didn't have hot water, and I'd been able to get it for two hundred fifty dollars a month versus three hundred seventy-five because of the *no hot water* thing. However, once the new water heater was installed, my rent was going up to three hundred seventy-five dollars. I also only had two more days before I was to show them my proof of renters insurance, which I did not have yet.

"If you'd like to take a day to think it over or perhaps meet my aunt first ..." the woman continued when I stayed silent.

"No—yes—I mean, yes, I'd like the job," I blurted out without even hearing what the pay was.

I'd just heard about the bedroom and agreed blindly. She had said it would pay better though. But honestly, even if it didn't, without the cost of rent and insurance to worry about, it didn't have to pay better. I would also be safe at night and could possibly sleep. Right now, I was too on edge to rest completely.

The woman smiled then, appearing to relax somewhat. Almost as if she'd been sent to find me, but that was silly. My father wouldn't do this. He wouldn't care enough. And Arthur, well, he'd manipulate things until I had to return.

"Seems my flat tire has turned out not to be bad luck after all," the woman said, then held out her hand to me. "I haven't even introduced myself. I'm Grissele Cash."

Cash? That name sent a surge of emotions through me. Even when used as a surname. Kash Savelle immediately rushed to the front of my thoughts triggering so many suppressed things. Memories of a time when life had been safe, when I'd felt alive, when all it had taken was one look from *him* and all was right in the world.

Wait … I knew that surname. Was she one of those Cashes? No, she wouldn't be related. I knew from my past that one of their women would never be left to wait on someone to change her tire if she had a flat. She'd have a driver slash bodyguard. And she would never have hired me to live with her aunt without a background check.

I wiped my hand on the apron I was wearing, afraid I'd get grease on her, then took hers to shake it. "Cressida Beck," I told her, impressed by the firm grip she had. I'd not expected that.

"It's nice to meet you, Cressida."

TWO

KASH SAVELLE

Twenty-Five Years Old

It wasn't like I was in college. Getting to go home for the holidays wasn't a thing. My life was in Alabama. I hadn't wanted it to be. But that wasn't my decision. I'd made the mistake, and now I had to pay the price. I was just so fucking tired of it.

Tossing my duffel onto the bed in my childhood bedroom, I sighed. I should be happy that my dad had called and asked me if I'd like to spend the holidays here. And I was. But leaving was going to be hard after being back.

Slowly, my gaze took in the room. Everything was the same—well, almost. There were a few changes. Mostly the photos. There was only one left of the ones I'd had in here. I walked over to pick it up. Crosby Cash's cocky grin made my chest tighten with sorrow. He had one arm thrown over my shoulders and another over my brother Forge's. Than Carver had taken the photo. We looked like normal teenage boys; we were anything but. Death wasn't something we feared until it was one of us that had been killed.

Since Crosby's death, it had been harder for me to take a life. Even when they fucking deserved it.

"Thought you were coming next week." My oldest brother's voice interrupted my memories, and I set the frame back down before turning to look at Oz.

He was leaning against the doorframe with his arms crossed over his chest and his brows drawn together. Damn, he was looking more like Dad, the older he got.

"Mom wanted me home earlier once she found out I was allowed to come," I replied.

Dad had told her on Thanksgiving because she had been down about my not being there. He had wanted to lift her spirits, but I doubted he had expected she'd demand that I come home immediately.

The corner of his lips quirked. "Her baby, back in his room."

"Don't be jealous that I'm the favorite," I drawled.

He chuckled. "Surprised you're staying here and not at Bane's."

"This is part of the deal. Dad said I had to stay here."

Forge lived at Bane's, and Oz had, too, until he married Winslet. Forge had been talking about moving into the Bowens' place, but he hadn't yet. Locke and Gathe Bowen had their own house, and neither of them was hooked up with a woman. Bane was married with a kid now, and life at his house wasn't what it used to be.

Oz straightened and dropped his arms to his sides. "Must be Mom's Christmas present this year. Having you under her roof."

I'd thought the same thing. Especially when I walked in the door and she wrapped her arms around me and held on to me for several minutes. In truth, getting to come back and stay for any amount of time felt like my Christmas present.

The last time I'd stayed here overnight was for Crosby's funeral, and that had only been one night before I had to go back. When I had come home for Oz's wedding, it had been a day trip.

"We're having a second Thanksgiving tomorrow, I hear. One where you're at the table too," Oz said. "Think you can talk her into something besides turkey and dressing? I had my fill already."

I laughed and shook my head. "I've not had her dressing in years. Suck it up. I want that and her corn casserole."

He groaned, then asked, "How's Bama?"

I shrugged. "Fine." Not Mississippi. Not home.

"I thought things were good there," he said as he studied me closely.

"They are."

We stood there silent for a moment. Oz was frowning as he waited for more. But I had nothing more to say about it.

"Doesn't sound like it's fine." Concern was now in his tone.

"It's not Madison. It'll never be home." Even after four years there, I still felt out of place. It was family, but not my family. I wanted to be here. I had grown up. I wasn't the same hotheaded kid anymore.

"What about Noble's daughter?"

Dwight Noble, head of the Alabama branch, would like his daughter, Jazz, to matter to me. We'd fucked, and I had tried to feel something for her. But she was so damn spoiled and whiny. It wore on my nerves. The fucking wasn't good enough to make the rest of the package bearable.

"Not a thing," I said. "We've fucked around, and she's clingy, but I've never promised more."

Oz cocked an eyebrow. "You're just fucking around with Noble's daughter?"

13

"Dixon fucked around with her before me. Except he wanted a relationship. She didn't. Noble doesn't care as long as she's fucking inside the family."

I wished she'd go back to Dixon. Maybe he'd stop sulking all the damn time.

"I can talk to Linc," Oz said. "About you possibly getting to stay. Come home for good. I'll take Bane with me."

I didn't want to get my hopes up about it. Linc Shephard was a hard-ass. Besides, he couldn't make the final call. The boss would have to do that, and Blaise Hughes wasn't one to change his mind.

"I doubt it will do much good," I told him.

"Things change. You might be surprised."

Oz walked over toward me, then wrapped an arm around my neck before pulling me in for a quick hug. "Glad you're home, little brother."

I was too. More than any of them would ever understand. They'd never been sent away. It was the loneliest feeling in the world.

THREE

CRESSIDA

I had forgotten what a full night of sleep felt like on a bed. Stretching as a smile spread across my face, I took in the bedroom that I still couldn't believe was mine. This all felt like a Christmas miracle. It had been a very long time since luck had landed on me. I had fallen asleep last night pinching myself, sure that this was all a dream. The pretty yellow and blue room, with the early morning sunlight filtering through the curtains, felt safe. Something I'd not experienced for a long time. The realization that the sun was rising hit me.

My eyes fell on the clock on the bedside table, and it was ten minutes to seven. Had I really slept that late? I had to hurry and get to the kitchen.

The schedule that Grissele had given me said that Glenda ate breakfast at seven thirty in the sunroom. Then, at eight thirty, she had a yoga class to attend at the local assisted living facility. Her day was rather packed, but then Glenda hadn't appeared elderly either. Sure, she had white hair cut in an elegant bob, but she got around rather well for eighty-three years old, and she was entertaining to talk to.

I made my way to the bathroom and quickly handled my morning routine before pulling on a pair of jeans and my nicest sweater. My wardrobe was limited. I'd taken only what I needed when I ran. Grissele hadn't mentioned a dress code, so hopefully, my wearing the same things often would be okay.

If I needed more clothes, with the pay I was getting from this job, I could buy them soon. My list of worries had been cut in half yesterday, thanks to my fairy godmother dropping into the diner. One minute, I'd been stressed over possibly being homeless, and the next, I was living in a nice big house on the other side of town, in a gated community.

Arthur wouldn't walk in the door here and force me to go back to my father's house. Even if he did try and find me.

Smiling at that thought, I headed for the door and down to the kitchen. I had already looked over Glenda's breakfast menu and knew what I needed to make for her. It was the same every morning but on Sundays. And seeing as today was Sunday, she would be having her splurge breakfast—or so she had called it.

Although I didn't think protein pancakes with ten chocolate chips and whipped cream on top was a splurge. But then, considering she had one slice of whole wheat toast, two scrambled eggs, and a cup of berries the rest of the week, then perhaps it was.

I had been shown where to find everything yesterday, so I went to work as soon as I entered the kitchen. It was a cheery place. All white and bright with a Christmas tree decorated in silver and blue, standing in the far corner, along with the scent of cinnamon lingering in the air from the wreath made of cinnamon sticks and white berries, which hung inside the large window beside the table. Tomorrow was the first day of December, but it seemed Glenda was one of those early decorators. There were three other Christmas trees in her house, stockings on the mantel, and other festive items placed throughout.

I went to work filling the water kettle and turning it on so it would be ready for her morning tea. She liked to have a pot brought out to her first before she had her breakfast, so that was a priority. Once I was done with that, I went about making the batter for her pancakes while humming "Jingle Bells."

"Alexa, play holiday music."

Glenda's voice startled me. I'd been so focused on the pancakes that I hadn't heard her enter the room.

My head snapped up, and I saw her smiling at me.

"Sounded like you were in the mood for some holiday tunes," she told me as she stood there, wrapped in a cream-colored velvet robe with fake fur trim around the collar.

"Yes. I didn't know you had one of those," I replied, glancing over toward where the sound was coming from. I didn't see the Alexa box though.

"It's hidden behind the poinsettias," she replied. "I don't like the look of the thing, but I can't live without it. When it's time to get groceries, ask her for the list. I tell her to add things to it all the time. She's a right helpful little thing."

"All I Want for Christmas" by Mariah Carey began to play over the hidden speaker.

"I didn't realize it did that too," I replied.

We had never had one in our home. My father was convinced the government controlled them and listened in on homes that had them. If anything, they were listening in on our phones. But I never argued that with him. I never argued anything with him. I had done my best to stay away from the man.

17

"Oh, yes. It also tells me the weather. I don't know how I ever lived without it."

I was going to ask it questions later. She had me intrigued.

"I have your hot water ready. Would you like me to make your tea?"

Glenda nodded. "Yes, please. I like to drink it in the sun-room," she told me. "I'd carry it in there myself, but the last time I tried, I spilled it and burned my hand terribly."

"That's what I'm here for," I assured her. "I will have it right out."

"Did you sleep all right? Was the bed comfortable?"

I wanted to laugh at that question. After where I'd been sleeping, any bed would have been comfortable. "It was wonderful. I haven't slept that well in months," I told her. It was more like years, but she didn't need my backstory.

Her smile grew. "That's good. If you need extra blankets or different pillows, just let me know."

"Everything is perfect," I assured her.

She nodded, seeming pleased, then turned to walk back out of the kitchen. I finished up the last pancake, then went to make her pot of tea.

FOUR
KASH

"I'm not fucking sharing with you so you can order three different things off the menu. Pick one and eat it," Forge said to Gathe, not looking up from his menu.

"I can't pick just one. Saylor and I always share," Gathe grumbled. "Kash? You want to share?"

"I hate mushrooms," I told him. "And I don't like the sound of the Sicilian sausage spaghetti."

Gathe sighed heavily. "Fine. I'll just take home the leftovers."

"I'd have thought by now that you'd be used to ordering meals without Saylor," Forge said as he put the menu down on the table and looked at Gathe.

Saylor had always been Crosby's girl, growing up, but everyone knew Gathe was her best friend. When Crosby had been killed and his secret came out—in the form of a baby momma who was not Saylor—I kind of thought she might end up with Gathe. I thought we all did. But instead, she had caused the local Catholic priest to sin, and Father Jude was no longer ordained. He was in the family business and engaged to Saylor.

Gathe shrugged. "I normally get someone to share with me if Saylor and Jude aren't here."

I glanced out the window across the street toward the church that sat up on the hill. I wondered if it felt odd for Jude to eat here with that view. Did he ever feel guilty?

My eyes scanned the rest of Main Street. It had been a while since I'd been in town. I'd already been home a little over a week. Time was moving too fast. I wanted it to slow the fuck down. When Christmas was over, I would have to leave, and I didn't want to. I wanted this life back. My depressing thoughts ceased as my gaze locked on the redhead. Long copper locks hung in a thick, wavy mass with lighter streaks running through it. I'd fucking know that hair anywhere.. My eyes dropped to her waist and ass. The sway of it, the shape, it was burned into my memory.

Cressida. She was in Madison. Why? How long? Did the family know? Why did I fucking care?! She was the reason I'd been sent away. She was the cause of all my problems. But then she always had been. From the moment I'd laid eyes on her, she had caused me nothing but turmoil. No, that wasn't true. I wanted it to be but it was a lie I told myself in order to keep sane.

Tearing my eyes off her before Gathe or my brother noticed who I was looking at, I set down the menu and tried to breathe normally, although my lungs were burning. Had I been holding my breath? Fuck, my hands were trembling. Jesus! It had been four years. What the hell was my problem?

The waitress appeared at the table, and I knew I needed to be alone and get myself together before my brother or Gathe realized something was wrong with me.

"I'll have the lasagna," I blurted out, then moved to get up. "I'll be back," I told both of them, then headed toward the back hall that led to the restrooms.

My heart was racing in my chest, like I'd been running a goddamn marathon. Dammit, why did I let her do this to me still? From the first time I had seen her standing in the hallway at school, lost and looking for her locker, I'd reacted like this.

I passed the restrooms, knowing where I was going and all the fucking reasons I should turn the hell around. But like so many times before, I had no control over my actions when it came to her. Cressida Beck triggered my crazy.

SEVEN YEARS AGO

"You coming or not?" Gathe called out to me from his truck.

We were supposed to meet the others at Proof Pony—a local bar—after football practice. My Hummer was in the shop, getting new rims, so I'd had to catch a ride to school with Gathe. He was the only one who passed my house every morning. Well, Crosby was close by, and it wouldn't be out of his way, but he'd have Saylor in the car with him, and I couldn't listen to her whine and bitch that early in the morning.

My eyes were locked on the black Mustang that had just pulled up near the entrance of the school. The owner of the car, Pirate Beck, wasn't of any interest to me, but his sister was a different story. Was he here to get her, and if so, why was she still at school?

One of the wide double doors swung open, and Cressida came out with her book bag tossed over her shoulder. The wind caught her hair, and it floated around her shoulders like fucking flames.

Damn, she was gorgeous.

It was becoming harder to stay away from her. She was too damn sweet, and she'd already dealt with shit in her life. I might keep my distance, but it didn't mean I hadn't run a background check on her. My obsession with the girl was just getting worse. She had only been here for a couple of months, but it was getting to the point that my day revolved around searching her out. I was close to putting a tracker on her, and I knew that was fucked up, but the need to know where she was might be stronger than my sanity.

She paused in her step when her gaze locked on mine. I liked how I made her nervous. She always licked her lips before her perfect white teeth bit down on her bottom lip. The hope in her eyes that I'd speak to her was so damn vivid that it was difficult to ignore.

One delicate, manicured hand lifted and waved at me. My mouth quirked as I fought back a smile. She was getting brave. That was new. The wave was bold. I liked it. Too much.

"Dude!" Gathe called out impatiently.

I held out a hand. "In a minute," I replied, not taking my eyes off her.

Fuck it. I was going to talk to her. She'd waved. I couldn't get in the damn truck and drive off.

The moment I headed in her direction, her eyes widened and brightened instantly. That wasn't going to help my good intentions. I was already picturing her face every time I fucked or got sucked off. That had pretty much started the moment I saw her.

She took a step toward me, then paused, as if she wasn't sure I was headed to her or not. Her eyes did a quick scan of the area around her to see she was alone, except for her brother—well, technically, he was her adopted brother, although her family said he was her stepbrother. I knew the truth. I'd read it in her file.

"Now, what kept you at school so late? Don't tell me you were in detention. I didn't peg you for a troublemaker," I said as I reached her.

Her eyes were back on me now, and she could not look more fucking adorable. All flustered and excited.

"No, I, uh, I'm in the school musical. I had to stay to work with the piano player and music teacher on one of the harder songs I'm singing."

I hadn't known there was a musical. Had they always had those? Wait, maybe I'd seen something about it, but I hadn't paid attention. That was about to change.

"You sing?" I asked.

Her cheeks pinkened, and she nodded her head.

"When is this musical?" Because I wasn't missing it.

"In two weeks," she replied hesitantly. "But I doubt you'd want to see it. I can't imagine *Mean Girls* is your thing?"

I had no idea what the fuck that was. "You onstage might be though." And that came out without me thinking it through.

Her breathing hitched, and it was obvious she was fighting back a smile. She didn't have to; her eyes said it all.

"Oh," she replied in a soft whisper.

Too sweet for you, Kash. You're not good for her. She needs someone who doesn't have a dark side.

"You should probably go. Your brother is waiting," I told her, not giving a shit about him, but trying to get her away from me because it was clear I wasn't able to do the right thing.

She nodded. "Yeah, he has work," she said. "Um, well, uh, bye."

"Have a good night," I told her and stepped back.

"You too," she said. Then, with one last look, she turned and hurried toward his car.

My hands tightened into fists at my sides at the way he was watching her. Waiting on her. I didn't want another guy taking her anywhere. Even if he was her brother. That was a major warning flag that I should pay attention to, but I feared I was about to ignore it.

FIVE

CRESSIDA

Present Day

I reached out to take Glenda's dry cleaning as the man passed it to me over the counter. This was a once-a-week errand. Every Tuesday, while she was at her bridge game, I took Glenda's clothes that needed to be cleaned to the dry cleaner and then picked up the clothes from the week before. I still had an hour before I had to go get her from her game, and she'd given me thirty dollars and told me to go buy lunch somewhere and relax. Going to a restaurant felt like a splurge, but then the Italian place, Vapiano's, was right across the street. That was tempting.

"Thanks," I told the man and took her clothing before heading out, planning to put it away in her Cadillac before deciding on where I would be eating.

Stepping out into the cool December air made me shiver. I needed to buy a coat. I should probably go to the second-hand store to do that instead of eating pasta. But if I didn't use the money she had given me for food, like she'd said, I'd feel guilty. I'd have to return it, and that would upset her. But then I could go buy a coat with my money and grab a sandwich somewhere to appease her. I glanced back down the street behind me, trying to remember where the secondhand store used to be.

Then I stumbled. Barely catching myself from face-planting on the sidewalk when my eyes met ones the color of the bluest ocean. My heart slammed in my chest so hard that it was painful, and I held Glenda's clothes to my chest like a lifeline as I stared at the one man who had not only been my world once, but also destroyed it—Kash Savelle.

"Hello, little Songbird," he said in his thick Southern drawl that had always made my knees weak.

Even after his actions had ruined my life, stolen my mother from me, left me alone, they still trembled. Damn my knees. Traitors.

"Kash." I tried to sound casual as I said it. As if seeing him again didn't affect me. I failed. My voice cracked, and my breathing came out in a hitch.

"Didn't know you were back in town," he said, appearing so unaffected by the sight of me that it hurt.

It shouldn't. It had been four years, and the last words he had spoken to me still sliced so deep that I couldn't allow them to resurface.

I cleared my throat in hopes of it not giving away what all I was feeling. "I, uh—yes, for about six months now."

His jaw ticced, and that was the only sign that he had any reaction to seeing me at all. Even if it was loathing or simply hate. He was excellent at masking his emotions. I'd forgotten about that.

"I thought you were in Alabama," I said, lifting my chin and straightening my shoulders.

He could despise me. I no longer cared. He'd not listened to me. Trusted me. Then he had ripped my life to

26

pieces in a way that I was still struggling to patch it back together.

"Home for the holidays," he replied in a clipped tone.

His gaze turned cold. Similar to the last night I'd seen him. A detachment that hadn't been there before. It haunted me in my dreams still.

"That's nice," I replied. "I'm sure your family is happy about that."

Because he had a family. One that loved him. Unlike me. I had no one.

I needed to go. Standing here with him staring at me that way again was too much. I had made progress in getting those shreds of myself back together, and being near him threatened that.

Kash Savelle was destruction. He'd once told me he didn't break pretty things, but he had shattered me.

"It was good to see you, Kash. Merry Christmas," I said, forcing a smile, then turned and hurried away before he said something that would make me stop or keep me there any longer.

My sole focus was getting to Glenda's car, getting inside it, and driving away. I'd find a coat another day. I could go through a drive-through for lunch. One that wasn't on Main Street. Maybe even one that wasn't in Madison.

SEVEN YEARS AGO

Words of praise surrounded me as I stood, holding the flowers that my mother had given me, along with pink roses that Pirate had handed me. I smiled and said my thank-yous, feeling as if I was on a high. But not because of my performance tonight. No, that wasn't it at all.

27

My euphoria had come from one single source. Kash had been here. My eyes met his while I sang the last song. He smiled at me and winked. He had come to see me. I knew he had. He hadn't even known about the musical until I told him. But then he had barely acknowledged me since that afternoon outside the school.

I scanned the crowd as I nodded my head and continued to thank those who spoke to me. My mom had said she'd have Pirate wait to take me home. There was a cast party I had to attend first. She and my dad were going to go ahead and leave.

As if the sea had parted, the people around me faded as Kash stepped into view. Voices fell away, and all I could see was him. The corner of his mouth lifted in a crooked grin as he walked toward me. My eyes drifted down his body to take in the sight he made when I realized he was holding flowers. But not any like I had seen before. The daisies, daffodils, and roses in my hands didn't compare to the round bouquet of bright orange and iridescent blue hues. They were stunning.

My eyes snapped back up to his just as he reached me.

"You came," I blurted out.

He chuckled. "Yeah, I did. Good thing, too, because now I know you have more than one superpower."

What? I frowned.

He leaned closer to my ear, and the scent of leather and spice sent a tingle through me. "Not only can you own a man with that face of yours, but you can claim his soul with that voice, little Songbird."

The warmth of his breath brushed my cheek just before his lips touched it gently, and then he straightened back up. Leaving me and taking his smell and heat with him. I wanted to reach out and grab his shirt and pull him back to me. Hold him close. Bask in how it felt.

"These are for you," he said, holding the flowers out to me.

I was completely reeling and wasn't sure if my legs were strong enough for the effect this man had on me as I reached to take them. "They're ... incredible," I said breathlessly, as if he'd just grabbed me and kissed me properly instead of just a simple peck on the cheek.

"Birds of paradise. I thought they fit you. Elegant and worth the wait."

SIX
KASH

Present Day

The license plate was burned into my brain. The silver Cadillac XT5 that Cressida had hastily tossed the dry cleaning into and then climbed in before speeding off looked like a mom car. I'd not allowed myself to check on her since I'd been sent to Alabama, and I didn't look at her ring finger. Dammit. That face of hers had had me so fucking mesmerized that I didn't do a proper check. She was even more gorgeous at twenty-three than she had been at nineteen, and I hadn't thought that was possible. Hell, I didn't even know what she'd been wearing. Was she married? A mom?

My gut clenched up and twisted as I stalked back to the restaurant, not bothering to enter through the back door, but going inside the front. Let them see me. The bastards knew she was back in town. The family knew everything, yet no one had mentioned it.

Forge's eyes met mine as I took long, purposeful strides to the table, and I did my best to remain calm. Act as if seeing her hadn't fucked my head up. Sure, I wanted to grab the chair I'd been sitting in and throw it through the goddamn window, but I wouldn't. I was past that now. I had learned to control my temper … or rather rage.

Pulling out my chair without force and sitting down, I felt both their eyes locked on me. Had they seen us out there? Possibly. Might as well clear the air.

"So, were either of you planning on telling me Cressida was back in town?" I asked, picking up my water to take a drink and looking from Gathe to my brother.

"Truth?" Forge asked as my eyes swung to him and narrowed. "No," he added. "I figured it was best that you didn't have a reminder. I'd like you to get to stay through Christmas. If you go and mess that up with Cressida, then it'll ruin Mom's Christmas."

The grip I had on my glass tightened, but I didn't let it show in my expression. I wasn't going to ruin anything over Cressida. But I wanted to fucking know if she was married with a kid. Playing soccer mom or some shit. NO! I didn't need to know. She wasn't mine. Not anymore. The only time I thought about her was when she appeared in my dreams, and that happened more often than not. Always little replays of her smiling, laughing, throwing her arms around my neck, whispering that she loved me in my ear.

FUCK! I set my glass down harder than necessary.

"She's my past. Four years. Can't we all let that go?" Especially me.

Forge nodded his head slowly. "Yeah. We did. That's not the problem. But can you?"

There was a time when I had let that girl own me. She'd had all of me. I'd been obsessed with her. Then she fucking blew up my goddamn chest with her betrayal. Nothing had ever been the same since that night. And not because I had killed the son of a bitch in her bed. I'd killed a lot of men. Cressida had demolished the only good inside me. Her. Loving her. She'd left me with the black soul I'd always had, and with it had come the misery.

"What I felt for her died the same night I killed her brother," I replied as the familiar ice slowly began to work its way through my veins.

"Good. Because here comes our food, and I'd like to eat without all the fucking tension," Gathe said with a smirk.

It must be easy for those two. They'd never loved a woman, never given their soul to one. I'd like to say if I could go back, I'd have stayed away from Cressida, but that would be a lie. Even knowing how it would end, I wouldn't erase it. The memories that were only allowed in my dreams were often how I survived another day.

SIX YEARS AGO

"What in the world?" Cressida said the words as she studied the portable building sitting in her front yard. It was covered in fairy lights and birds of paradise.

"Happy birthday, little Songbird," I said, walking up behind her and sliding my hands around her waist to hold her against me.

She jumped, startled at first since she hadn't known I was here, but instantly sank back against my chest.

"I thought you had to go to a horse race?" she said, her tone going soft and breathy as I pressed a kiss near her ear.

"I lied," I told her. "And I can't believe you bought it. I'd never fucking leave you on your birthday."

"Oh," she said as a smile curled her lips. "When you woke me up just before dawn, calling and asking me to go look outside, I expected balloons or maybe flowers …"

"That's too basic," I said as I wrapped a strand of her hair around my finger.

"So, you got me ... what exactly?" Her tone was hesitant.

"Go inside and see," I said, letting her hair go and gently pushing her toward the door.

A soft giggle came from her, and what I really wanted to do was pick her up and haul her off. Keep her locked away with me.

I reached around her and turned the knob. "Go in quickly," I said.

"Oookay," she replied, sounding unsure.

I followed behind her, closing the door.

Twinkling lights and flowers filled the room, along with white butterflies.

"Oh my God!" She spun around and stared up at me, wide-eyed. "Butterflies!"

I nodded. "You said, as a little girl, you spent hours chasing butterflies, but never caught one. I thought it was time you did. So, I brought them to you." I pointed to the center of the room. "Go stand there and be still. No chasing required. They'll come to you."

She blinked as her eyes began to water. "You ... you did all this so I could hold a butterfly? There has to be at least a hundred of them in here!"

"One hundred forty-nine, to be exact. That's how many days it's been since our first date," I told her.

She sniffled, and a smile spread across her face as one tear broke free and rolled down her cheek. "Really?"

"Yeah, but I kinda hoped I wasn't the only one who knew that number's significance."

She laughed, and her eyes danced with amusement. "I knew. I was asking if that was really how many butterflies were in here."

I nodded. "I counted to be sure."

Instead of going to the middle of the room, she threw her arms around my neck, going up onto her tiptoes to do so. I had to take her waist and lift her so that she could bury her nose in the curve of my neck, the way she loved to do.

"I love you," she whispered and pressed a kiss to my warm skin.

"You'd better. Because you own me."

SEVEN

CRESSIDA

Present Day

Kash might have exited my life, but he remained in my dreams. However, since I'd run into him on Tuesday, he'd starred in every dream I had the last two nights. If there was a way to make it stop, I would. Thinking about him was something I had trained myself not to do, and it had taken almost two years. But that had all been shot to hell, it seemed.

Throwing myself into preparing for the holiday tea party that Glenda was hosting for her friends had been a little distraction. I cleaned the place until it shone, prepped all the dishes she had wanted, and pulled recipes from online. Although she had told me she would have it catered, I'd insisted that I wanted to do it all. I needed to. Otherwise, I would be staring at a book every evening once Glenda went to bed at seven, pretending to read it while all I did was replay the few words Kash had said.

Glenda's guest arrived today at two. Once that was over and I cleaned up, what was I going to use to keep myself busy at night? Maybe I could buy some cheap earbuds and listen to free audiobooks. I had the money to buy them, but I wanted to save every dime I could. I never knew what the future held, and I wanted to eventually have my own security of a vehicle and savings.

Saturdays were my day off, and I dreaded this next one. Glenda always left with Grissele in the mornings and didn't return until it was time for her to bathe and go to bed. Although Glenda always left me her car and encouraged me to go do something for myself, I never did. I had nowhere to go. I normally read a book in the sunroom, walked around her neighborhood for an hour to get in some exercise, and watched a movie.

"This place has never been cleaner," Glenda said as she walked into the sunroom.

I was finishing setting up the tables with the holiday china and turned to look at her. She was wearing a green sweater with snowflakes on it and a white pencil skirt that hit mid-calf. The festive sight she made caused me to smile.

"You look lovely," I told her.

She placed a hand on her hip and posed for me. "Well, thank you," she said. "I've been waiting for an occasion to wear this sweater. I bought it on a clearance sale last year after Christmas. One can never turn down a luxurious chenille piece when it's sixty percent off."

I was sure that Glenda could afford it at the normal price tag, but she wasn't one to waste money. She liked a good deal, and if there was a sale in town, she was going to find it.

"And green is your color," I replied. "It shows off your eyes."

She wiggled her eyebrows with a smirk. "Well then, I might just need to go buy some more of it."

I decided then that I knew exactly what I would get her for Christmas. A scarf in that exact color. For Glenda, I would splurge.

The oven timer dinged.

"That's the rose zucchini tartlets," I said. "I'll go get those out and put in the spinach puff pastry Christmas trees."

"Oh, I can't wait to see and taste those," Glenda replied as I left the room.

The only thing I hadn't made for today was the yule log. There was a bakery in town where Glenda always bought from, and I knew if I tried, I couldn't make one like that. It was centerpiece-worthy. I was happy with how all the rest that I had made turned out. I'd spent a few evenings doing some trials and had to look up how to successfully make the puff pastry on YouTube, but I had succeeded eventually.

This was the first Christmas I had enjoyed in a very long time. Only my earlier years with my parents were happy memories. I struggled to remember a time that Pirate hadn't ruined the holiday for us. He had always been difficult. Even at a young age I had tried my best to handle him to keep the family peace, but near the end, he'd gotten worse. He had started to scare me—

No! I wasn't thinking about that. I'd talked about it all I ever wanted to in therapy. My mother had sent me to a counselor three days a week until her death. My father had canceled it, saying it was a waste of time.

Opening the stove, I pulled out the tartlets, and they were perfect. Sighing in relief, I placed them on the stone countertop and went to take the puff pastry Christmas trees from the refrigerator. Once these were done, all would be baked. I just had to begin placing things on the food buffet in the sunroom.

Glancing at the clock, I checked the time. We had forty minutes before guests would arrive.

A ding from the cell phone that Grissele had given me went off, and I stared at it for a moment, where I'd left it on the far end of the counter. Who would be texting me? Glenda was here, and Grissele would just call her if she needed her. I didn't use the phone for anything other than having it on hand for Glenda when I was running errands or waiting on her while she was at one of her appointments.

It made the sound again, and I walked over to it, deciding that maybe Grissele needed me to do something before she arrived. But the strange number on the screen wasn't hers. It had to be a wrong number or spam. I'd gotten those back when I had a phone. But this was the first time it had happened with this phone.

Picking it up, I tapped it since there was no lock on the phone. I had no reason to lock the screen.

> Don't speak to or make any contact with Kash. This is your only warning.

The phone slipped from my grip and clattered onto the countertop. I stared at it. A million different things running through my head. How? Who? Why? But deep down, I knew. This might be a rarely used phone that wasn't under my name, but they could find out anything. I'd been worried when I returned that they might not want me here, but I'd heard nothing. Seen none of them. Until Tuesday, and it would have to be Kash that I saw.

The Southern Mafia owned this town; it owned the South. And I was on their radar even though I'd lied to save Kash four years ago. Done it without thought before they could even ask me to. But they didn't trust me. Kash was one of them. I wasn't.

My hands were trembling as I stood frozen.

"It sure smells delicious in there!" Glenda's cheery voice called out.

I had to get myself together. Make it through this day. I'd think about the text tonight. Figure out what this meant for me here. Could I stay? Tears pricked my eyes, and I fought them back. Not now. I couldn't fall apart now.

The click of Glenda's low-heeled shoes drew closer, and I took a deep breath, then let it out. I was fine. I'd done nothing wrong. No need to overreact. I glanced at the phone again. Should I respond? Would whoever that was think I was ignoring them if I didn't?

Jerking up the phone, I quickly typed out.

> I have no desire to. I was in town, getting dry cleaning for my employer. Kash spoke to me. It was a short conversation, and I left. I'm not here for Kash. I just need to start a new life.

I reread it three times, then hit Send. Whoever that went to, I hoped this was enough to keep them away from me.

EIGHT
KASH

Nothing? What the fuck?

"How is there nothing on Cressida Beck?" I demanded.

Ted didn't work for the family exactly. He was more of a criminal, who was also a computer genius that we used for anything we didn't want the family to know we were doing. And when I said *we*, I meant the younger members of the Mississippi branch. Sometimes, there were things we kept from our fathers and Linc.

"Dude, like I said, it's like she doesn't exist. I can't find shit, and that never happens," he replied.

"That's impossible. I ran a background check on her seven years ago," I told him.

"I'll keep trying, but someone has her information blocked. Or the power to wipe it clean."

Who would have that kind of power, and why?

The family.

Motherfucker.

"What about the license plate number?" I asked.

"That is registered to a Glenda Spencer. She lives in Madison. I'll text you her address. But she's, like, eighty-three years old, man. Has no relation to a Cressida Beck."

"Who is Glenda Spencer related to? The name is familiar." I'd heard it before.

"Give me a sec," he said.

I sat silently, waiting as I listened to the sound of his typing.

"Ah, well, I'll be damned," Ted said, sounding amused.

My grip on the steering wheel tightened. I was prepared to not like what he was about to tell me.

"Glenda Spencer has one niece—Grissele Cash."

Aunt Glenda. I didn't need her address. I'd been to her house more than once with Crosby.

Putting on my blinker, I moved to the turning lane. Seemed it was time I went for a visit.

"Keep trying to get Cressida's background check," I told him before ending the call.

I made a U-turn, not caring that it was illegal at that stoplight. It was the least of the crimes I'd done in my life. My phone dinged, and I glanced down to see the address that Ted had sent me. Aunt Glenda hadn't moved.

It wasn't a fucking coincidence that Cressida was in Aunt Glenda's Cadillac. Whatever the fuck my dad, Fender, and Linc were up to, I didn't like them messing with Cressida's life.

Why had she been in Glenda's car? How had they connected the two? What other family did Glenda have? Was there a grandson or nephew I didn't know about? Was Cressida with him? Did everyone know but me?

I stopped at the next red light as my internal battle waged on. My going to Glenda's would get back to Linc. I'd likely be sent to fucking Alabama before nightfall. But they were keeping something from me. And Cressida was involved. What if she'd gotten married or was with some other guy?

My chest felt so goddamn tight that I had to rub it. FUCK! Why did I still care? She should be dead to me. What was it going to take to get her out of my head? I wanted my life back, here in Madison. And I'd gotten a chance to maybe convince everyone I was good to come home, and she had shown up.

When the light turned green, I didn't go straight. I wasn't messing this up. I had to move on with my life and let this shit with Cressida go. I turned right and headed toward the Carvers' distillery instead. Gathe was there. He'd texted me to meet him and Than for lunch, but I'd ignored it because I was waiting to hear what Ted had found out on Cressida.

Time to change my focus. Get my head straight again.

Than slid another bottle of whiskey across the table toward me. "Damn, it's good having you home," he said, picking up the glass he had just filled and taking a drink.

"Ain't that the truth?" Gathe said with a slur.

We'd been drinking for a few hours now. It started with a game of Texas Hold'em and moved to a game of pool, and then we'd ordered burgers and kept drinking.

"Seems the only way we get Than over here for a guys' night is having you here," Gathe added.

"That's not true," Than replied.

"Yeah, it fucking is," Forge said, walking back into the room with a bag of chips.

"No it isn't! I was at Bane's for the Egg Bowl," he argued.

"That doesn't count. You also had Montana on your lap," Forge shot back at him.

"All the women were there, not a guys' night," Gathe pointed out.

Than shrugged then. "Well, Six is prettier than the two of you."

Six was his nickname for Montana, his fiancée.

"You're pussy-whipped," Gathe told him.

Than nodded. "Abso-fuckin'-lutely I am. Completely obsessed with her."

I opened the bottle and filled my glass. I was glad Than was happy, but hearing how happy his woman made him brought back shit I was trying to shove away. Lock up. Forget.

"It's almost nine o'clock, and you've had me for six hours," Than said, taking another drink. "But Six will be home from her Christmas shopping trip soon."

Gathe groaned. "Leaving before ten? The night is young."

"And once I leave, the three of you can move this party to the strip club."

He had a point. That would be a distraction.

"Good idea." Gathe nodded.

"I'm in, but none of us needs to drive," Forge replied.

"Where's Locke?" I asked, realizing that we'd left the distillery and come to Gathe and Locke's place and Locke hadn't been home during that time.

"With Ransom and Oz. They're handling a bet that is overdue. Oz is collecting this week, and they've got one that's over five mil unpaid," Gathe said.

Oz handled the gambling side of the business. He'd been the bookie for the Mississippi branch for years. Not a job I'd want. But my brother was good at it. Only once had he almost lost a large amount, and he abducted the man's sister to draw him out of hiding. But while he was holding her captive, he had gotten obsessed with her. She was now my sister-in-law.

"Who went with the girls shopping then, Bane?" Forge asked before shoving a chip in his mouth.

"And Father Jude," Than added.

"What's he gonna do? Pray for them?" I asked, smirking as I took a drink.

"Jude's gotten pretty damn good with his Glock," Than said.

"I've been working with him," Gathe added, leaning back in his chair.

"Well, I'm sure he's lethal then," I replied with a roll of my eyes.

Forge burst out laughing and sank down on the sofa.

"You're all assholes," Gathe grumbled and took another drink.

This was what I'd missed. It wasn't the same in Alabama. The guys there weren't the ones I'd grown up with and trained with. I wanted this back. Not going to Glenda's today had been smart.

My text sound went off, and I pulled my phone out of my pocket.

Butler: Missing Bama yet?

Out of all the guys in Alabama, Butler was who I'd gotten close to. Dixon and I had been tighter once, but my fucking Jazz had made things different. I'd not realized it would at the time. Jazz was annoying at best. I hadn't known he had a real thing for her.

Me: Eh, not exactly. It's good to be home.

He'd been joking. He had known I wanted to go back to Mississippi. He understood. He'd feel the same if he had to leave Alabama.

"You got a piece of ass back in Bama?" Gathe asked.

I shook my head. "No. I don't do anything clingy. Too much work."

"Right?"

Watching the others all hooked up looked boring as fuck. At least that was what I was going to keep telling myself.

"Keep talking. It's coming for you one day," Than said, grinning like he knew something we didn't.

But I did. I knew. I'd felt that way about a girl once. Nothing came before her. She had been all I lived for. And when it was ripped from you, it was excruciating pain. He didn't know about that. Only I did.

My phone went off again, and I looked down at it.

Butler: Dixon and Jazz started fucking again. That's good news for you. At least she'll leave you alone. Other than that, the only thing happening here is Mullens knifed a dude at the Doghouse last night for mouthing off. Guy ended up being the Baptist preacher's son.

This wasn't unusual. Mullens had a temper and a mean streak. I'd had to get him off folks more than once so we didn't have a messy cleanup. He'd seen his father killed when he was five, and Butler had said he was never the same after. Messed him up in the head.

I didn't want to respond right now because I just didn't care. I wanted to forget Alabama for the time being and just enjoy this. Being where I belonged.

NINE

CRESSIDA

Six Years Ago

"You ready to go?" Kash asked, leaning down close to my ear.

I turned my head so that I could look up at him. "If you are."

These were his friends and their place. I was just happy to be with him, although having him alone was my favorite. Older girls, college-aged, were hanging on the other guys around our table, and the way they looked at Kash made me uncomfortable. I didn't like it, but he kept his arm around my shoulders and me tucked close to his side, never once acknowledging any other female. Well, except Saylor. She was with Crosby though and didn't feel like a threat.

"If I get to keep you another hour, I'd rather have you all to myself," he replied.

I hated my curfew. It was a Saturday night, and I wanted to stay out later, but my parents had insisted I be home by ten.

I nodded. "Yeah. I'm ready to go."

He winked at me, then stood up, holding out his hand for me to take. I slipped mine in his and followed him by standing.

"Y'all leavin'?" Crosby asked.

"Yeah," Kash replied.

"You comin' back after you take her home," Than said it more like a statement than a question.

"No," Kash told him, draping his arm over my shoulders. "Night," he said to all of them with a nod.

"I'm about to head out too," Forge said.

"Not going with us," Kash told his older brother as we began to walk away.

Several of the girls called out, "Bye," to Kash, and one told him to call her, but he didn't respond or even glance their way.

It was still difficult to listen to. Although Kash never made me feel as if I had any cause to worry that he might prefer someone else, I still felt as if this fairy tale I was living in, where the handsome prince had chosen me, would be snatched away at any time.

When we stepped outside, I wanted to sigh in relief. Kash stopped walking and turned his head to look down at me. He placed a finger under my chin and tilted my head back slightly. When our eyes locked, his brows drew together with concern.

"You know I'd never call another girl. I've got no fucking interest in any of them. I just see you."

This wasn't the first time he'd said this to me when we left somewhere that other females had openly hit on him. But it was good to hear. It made all the fear fade away, and I became warm and tingly.

"Yes," I replied. Because I did know that.

Even if I got insecure at times, I trusted Kash.

47

"Good," he said in a husky whisper as he began to lower his head for a kiss.

"You got some cash?"

The deep slur stopped him.

We both turned to see a man walking up to us from the parking lot. Although he sounded as if he might be drunk, he wasn't staggering as he approached. When he stepped into the light, I moved back slightly. His eyes looked weird with large pupils, and his long hair was pulled back in an oily ponytail. When they went from Kash to me, a creepy smile spread across his face.

"Well, ain't she a pretty thing you got there?"

I wanted to go back inside now.

Kash moved in front of me, and I started to reach out and grab his hand to tug him away. I didn't want that man hurting him. But before I could even touch him, he took two long strides toward the man and pulled a gun from beneath his leather jacket.

What the heck?!

"Whoa!" the man said, staggering back as Kash pressed the gun to the man's forehead. "I just needed some money, man."

"You looked at what's mine."

Kash's tone made me shiver, and I crossed my arms over my chest as I watched the scene, no longer recognizing the boy I loved.

"Kash"—Forge's voice came from behind me—"what's the problem?"

"This fucker looked at her," he snarled, keeping the gun to the man's head.

The man held up both his arms. "I-I'm sorry. I didn't know."

I swung my gaze from Kash to Forge. He appeared relaxed and not at all shocked by Kash having a gun and pointing it at someone's head.

Forge sighed heavily, as if annoyed. "Let the man go," he told Kash. "We don't want a cleanup job over some shit like that."

Kash tilted his head slightly, as if he was studying the man in front of him. "You're gonna turn around and get the fuck out of here. Don't come back. I don't want to see your face again."

The man nodded. "I will. I mean, I'll go, and I won't come back."

For a moment, no one moved, and I was beginning to think Kash had changed his mind.

But then he lowered the gun and used it to point at the darkness. "Go."

The man stumbled backward, not taking his eyes off Kash before spinning around and running. He tripped almost immediately but kept from face-planting by catching himself with his hands. Clumsily, he stood back up and started running again.

Kash slid his gun back beneath his jacket, where he had pulled it from, and waited until the man was out of sight before turning around.

"Did he touch her?" Forge asked.

"No," Kash clipped out while glaring at his brother.

"What the fuck, man? You can't put a gun to a man's head over looking at her."

Kash's jaw ticced, and his eyes narrowed. "I didn't ask you, did I?"

Forge shook his head, as if exasperated. Still, he didn't seem at all concerned that his younger brother had a gun.

"Jesus," he muttered, then started off into the parking lot.

Kash's gaze cut to me and immediately softened. "You okay?" he asked.

"No, you scared the shit out of her," Forge called out as he continued walking away.

The concern in his gaze was nothing like the coldness that had been there when he turned around. "Fuck," he muttered and quickly closed the space between us. "I'm sorry," he told me as he cupped my face with his hand. "I didn't think about how that would upset you. I should have."

I blinked up into his beautiful face. I'd always known there was a darkness in his eyes at times. But I hadn't thought … well, I hadn't thought that it meant he was dangerous. Was he? Pirate had warned me that I should keep my distance from Kash, but I'd ignored him. Did he know something that I didn't?

He brushed my lower lip with the pad of his thumb. "I don't like anyone looking at you. I know what they see and what they're thinking. I don't like it. You're mine."

When I shivered this time, it wasn't from fear but the deep timber in his voice when he said I was his. I had never wanted anything more.

"You … you have a gun," I said before he made me forget everything I'd just witnessed.

He sighed. "Yeah, little Songbird, I do. There're some things about me you don't know. It's probably time I tell you. But I need you to promise me that it won't change the way you feel about me."

Nothing could change that, I realized. Even after what I witnessed, I wasn't scared of him. I wanted to get in his truck and go down to the lake he always took me to so we could be alone. It was where he'd first touched me. Taken off my clothes. It was where he'd taken my virginity. Where he'd told me he loved me.

"I love you," I said honestly. "That will never change."

The corner of his mouth lifted. "That's good, baby."

PRESENT DAY

My eyes flew open, as if someone had said my name. The room was dark still. It wasn't morning yet. I glanced at the clock on the bedside table to see it said three fifteen. I felt it then. The presence in the room.

Turning over, I sat up quickly, and my eyes began to scan the darkness. When they landed on the figure sitting in the chair to the right of the bed, I covered my mouth to muffle my scream. Because I knew that face. I'd been dreaming about him.

Was I still asleep? I had to be. He couldn't be in my bedroom in the middle of the night.

"You still talk in your sleep." That familiar voice soothed me, although I knew it shouldn't.

I slowly removed my hand from my mouth as I stared at him. This felt real. Like I was awake. But how could I be?

"Kash." I whispered his name.

"You know any other fucker who could sneak into your bedroom at night so successfully?"

No. Only him.

"Wh-what are you doing here?"

He smirked. "Hell if I know. I'm a stupid motherfucker. I'll blame it on the whiskey."

"How did you find me?"

A low chuckle filled the silence. "Come on now, Songbird. You know that answer. Did you think you could hide from me? Right under my nose at that."

I shook my head. "I wasn't—I mean—I …" I stammered, not sure what I was trying to say.

His words confused me. Had he meant my living in Madison again?

He leaned forward, resting his elbows on his knees. "Why don't you start with telling me why you're living at Aunt Glenda's?"

Aunt? I frowned.

"What?"

"You heard my question."

"Aunt ... Glenda?" I repeated hesitantly.

He nodded his head. "Not my aunt exactly. She's Bane and"—he paused for a moment—"Crosby's great-aunt."

Cash. Bane and Crosby Cash. *Oh my God.*

"Grissele ..." I said her name slowly.

"Yeah. What about Grissele?" he asked.

He knew her.

That meant, "She's Bane and Crosby's mother," I said, guessing the truth.

He nodded. "Yep. Now, why're you living at her aunt's house?"

I stared at him in shock. "I ... I don't know," I whispered, trying to put everything together in my head.

Had Grissele known who I was that day in the diner? Was this a coincidence? Or not?

"Let me ask this another way," he drawled. "How do you know Glenda?"

"I ... I work for her. I'm her sitter. I take her places. When you saw me Tuesday, I was getting her dry cleaning."

His scowl deepened. "Why are you in Madison, working as a sitter for an old lady? You were in college, getting your music degree. Why aren't you doing something with it?"

Because my life had fallen apart, along with my family, when he killed Pirate. But he didn't get to know all that.

"Things changed," I said simply.

"Why are you working here?" His tone was demanding.

I wasn't afraid of him, but I *was* afraid of the family.

"Grissele hired me. She had come to the diner I was working at and offered me the job. I didn't know who she was." Or I'd never have taken this job.

"When?"

"The Saturday after Thanksgiving."

He let out a humorless laugh and shook his head. "Bastards," he muttered. "The day before I got here. They didn't trust me."

He wasn't talking to me—at least, it didn't seem like it.

"So, she knew who I was when she came to the diner?"

He nodded. "Yeah, she knew. Grissele wouldn't have offered this job to some stranger in a diner. This is her only living relative other than her immediate family. Her parents are dead, and Glenda is all she has left of that side of her family. You were placed here so that the family could watch you while I was in town." He shook his head again and leaned back.

"Why are you back in Madison?" he asked me then.

I wasn't telling him that.

"Because I needed a new start. I …" Pausing, I thought about what I was comfortable telling him because I had to give him some reason or he'd keep asking me. "It was time I moved out of my father's house. My stepmother didn't want me there, and I didn't want to be there."

"Your parents divorced?"

I stiffened. "My mother is dead."

For a moment, there was a flicker of pain in his eyes. "I'm sorry. What happened? Was she sick?"

Yes, but not the way he meant.

"She drowned," I told him, not wanting to give him the details.

We sat in silence for a few moments. The text from earlier today came back to me, and panic tightened my throat.

"You need to leave," I told him. "I got a text earlier, warning me to stay away from you. I didn't know how they had my number since it's a phone that I only use for contact with Glenda when she needs me. But I guess that's cleared up."

He stood. "Where's the phone?" he asked.

I pointed to the dresser across the room.

He immediately went over to it. "What's the password?"

"I don't lock it."

He opened it up and began tapping at things and going through it. "Fuckers," he muttered. "They're tracking you."

I didn't ask who. I knew.

"It doesn't matter. All I do is go places for Glenda."

"Where's your other cell phone?"

"I don't have one."

He lifted his gaze to look at me. "You don't have a personal phone?"

I shook my head.

"What happened to your phone before you took this job?"

I crossed my arms over my chest and straightened my back. "I didn't have one," I replied tightly.

"Why?"

"I don't see how that is any of your business."

He narrowed those damn eyes of his at me again, and I mimicked his expression.

"How do you contact friends, your dad? There are no texts on here other than Glenda, Grissele, and the one you deleted that was sent from Bane's cell. I'll deal with him later."

Telling him why I didn't talk to my father or have friends wasn't happening either.

"I don't."

"Why?"

"Again, not your business."

His nostrils flared as he looked at me, and I could tell I was pissing him off, but I didn't care. He set the phone down, then grabbed the chair and moved it under the air vent.

"What are you doing?" I hissed, afraid his moving furniture would wake up Glenda.

"Looking for cameras," he replied standing in the chair. He took the vent cover off and began feeling around inside.

"Cameras?" I asked, my eyes going wide.

He put the cover back on. "Yes, cameras," he replied, then moved over to inspect a lamp shade, the curtains, and the light fixture.

I just watched silently in horror.

"At least they didn't invade your private space. There will be cameras in other areas of the house though. Hopefully, I wasn't caught on one."

He turned to look back at me.

"Do you like working for Glenda?"

I nodded. "Yes, I do. Very much." I liked the security that I felt, although it had been snatched away from me in a matter of minutes.

"Fine. Then stay. I'll … handle it."

"What do you mean by handle it?" I asked him.

He cocked an eyebrow at me. "Exactly what it sounds like. I'll find out who placed you here. And make sure you don't get any more fucking threatening texts."

"I didn't come back here for you, if they think that's why I'm here. I came for other reasons. I thought you were in Alabama."

His jawline grew sharper as he clenched his teeth. We said nothing while staring at each other a moment more before he started for the door. He was leaving. Relief should come with that, but there was the urge to call him back. Ask him to stay. I wouldn't do that though. He needed to go for both our sakes.

The door opened and closed silently. He was gone. The room felt colder than before.

TEN

KASH

The strip club we had frequented long before we were of legal age hadn't changed much. Sure, the dancers were new for me, but other than that, it was the same. This wasn't a job that had longevity. It was a high-end establishment, and their requirements for the dancers were hard to meet once they passed their mid-twenties or got knocked up.

Gathe had wanted to come tonight because he had a thing for one of them. I needed to get my thoughts off Cressida and what I'd learned in her room last night. I hadn't confronted Bane about the text he'd sent her, simply because I was afraid I'd be back in Alabama before nightfall. Since I'd made it all day without Linc calling me out, I hadn't been caught on any of the hidden cameras they had planted in Glenda's house. That was a relief. Truth was, if they ordered me to go back to Bama before Christmas, I wasn't sure I would obey. And that was concerning.

There was a lot Cressida hadn't told me last night, and it was driving me fucking crazy. Like, for example, why was she in Madison, working as a sitter for the elderly? I liked Aunt Glenda, but Cressida was too talented to be doing that. She'd had specific goals, dreams of starting a theater arts program for kids. One that was open to all kids, with scholarships for those who couldn't afford it. I'd loved to sit and listen to her talk about her ideas. And of all the different scenarios I'd imagined for her over the past four years, what she was doing now had never been one of them. I wished I didn't care. It would make life easier. But I did, and that was the fucking problem.

"You're quiet tonight," Forge said, eyeing me as he took a drink from the bottle of beer he'd ordered.

I shrugged. "What do you want me to say? We're looking at tits and ass. Should I comment on them?"

He wasn't amused.

"She's up next," Gathe told us, not taking his eyes off the stage. "Just wait till you see her tits. They look so fucking good with my cum all over them."

"Yeah, that's what I want to be thinking about while she dances," I drawled.

He glanced back at me and smirked. "I marked my territory. Thought you should know."

I wasn't interested. But we both knew if I was, I'd be able to snatch her away if I wanted to. We'd played that game when we were younger, and I'd always won.

"Yeah, you keep telling yourself that," Forge told him. "Pretend that she doesn't take other guys back to the private rooms to shoot loads on her tits."

Gathe narrowed his eyes at my brother. "How do you know?"

Forge rolled his eyes. "Don't be naive."

"Can I get you men another round?" a topless server with platinum-blonde hair that hung down over her shoulders and past her tits asked.

The silver lace thong she was wearing barely covered her cunt, and my brother did a slow take of her body before answering.

"Still finishing this one, darlin'," he drawled. "But you can sit in my lap."

She didn't hesitate, but looked excited at the idea. It wasn't that way with all the patrons, and honestly, it wasn't because of how Forge looked. They all knew. Who we were. What we did. And the danger and power made all their pussies wet. It was how we had been let in the doors before we were of legal age. I'd gotten my first blow job by a girl in my eighth-grade class, but I'd finished in my first mouth here. With one of the strippers on my fifteenth birthday.

The girl sat down on Forge's leg and spread her legs, glancing from him to me since I was the one getting the view of her open pussy lips now that the thin strip of fabric was between them.

Forge slid his hand between her thighs, getting close enough that he was almost touching it. I shook my head and smirked at his blatant disregard for the club rules, then went back to looking at the stage.

"I'm available if you boys want to go to a room," she said with a purr.

Yeah, I didn't double team with my brother.

"Depends on what you're willing to do for me," Forge told her. "I like it dirty."

"Why don't you let me show you? I can be a very bad girl."

"It'll just be the two of us. I don't share fucks with my brother, and that one has a hard-on for the next dancer."

I glanced back over at them to see she was rubbing her cunt on his thigh in a way that was making her tits bounce.

"Then I'll make it extra dirty," she promised.

"Sold," Forge replied, then cupped her pussy and squeezed, making her moan. "Lead the way."

She stood, and he followed but shot me a cocky grin first. She was about to take it up the ass with his giant dick. Hope she realized that. I shook my head and chuckled as they walked off.

"Guess that means we aren't getting refills," Gathe said.

"Not from that one," I replied.

"She did get my cock hard with the pussy rubbing she was doing, but not enough for me to miss Topaz," he said, turning his gaze back to the two dancers leaving the stage.

"Topaz," I replied. "How original."

"Shut up," Gathe shot back at me with a scowl.

"What's her real name?"

He shrugged. "Don't care."

"So, it's nothing more than physical, this obsession you have with her," I asked.

The look he had on his face answered that for me. "I like to fuck her mouth and come on her tits. That doesn't mean I want her to have my babies."

Maybe Gathe would be safe from being truly broken by a woman. I fucking wished I hadn't been. Once one claimed your soul, you were never the same. You couldn't ever get it back, not completely. She'd become part of it.

Topaz took the stage, and Gathe was locked in on her. I tried to be distracted by her, but I found myself reaching for my phone and staring down at the screen. I'd fixed the tracking device on Cressida's phone so that my number wouldn't be traced or recorded when I texted or called her. She didn't know that though. My texts would automatically delete once she read them too. I shouldn't have done it because it only added to the temptation to contact her.

"You look thirsty," a female said.

I lifted my gaze to see a new server in a hot-pink thong with matching stilettos and D-size tits in front of me. As I stared at them, the full pink nipples hardened. She was a distraction, and I needed one real damn bad right now.

Raising my eyes to her face, I gave her a slow grin. "What about you, sugar? Are you thirsty?"

She shimmied her hips slightly as she smiled at me. "For you? Very."

The owner must be sending them over to us. I'd leave a good tip tonight.

"Then why don't you take me somewhere and show me just how much?"

She bit her lower lip and did the shy thing that she'd clearly perfected. "Yes, sir."

Standing, I stepped closer to her until her tits brushed my chest. "Let's go."

The girl spun around and began her saunter back toward the private rooms. I admired her ass as she did, which was exactly what she had been hoping for. If I bent her over and took her from behind, I wouldn't see her face. I could imagine another face. Which wouldn't be the first time.

She passed three doors before stopping at an open one and turning back to me to wave me inside. I walked past her and waited until the door clicked shut behind her before taking my gun from its holster and placing it beside me on the small sofa table. I then began unzipping my pants. No use in having her dance for me. I'd have to look at her face then.

"Why don't we start with you on your knees?" I told her as I shoved my jeans down and freed my semi-hard dick.

Her gaze flickered to my gun, then back to me. There was a spark of excitement in her eyes. Maybe she got off on guns. I'd had more than one woman want me to fuck them with it. The only reason I'd even fucked Jazz the first time was that she had wanted me to rub the barrel of my gun around her nipples until she got off. She did so pretty quickly and squirted while she did it. That had been some wacked shit, but I'd come hard in her cunt after it.

"Only if you promise to gag me," she replied seductively.

I smirked. That was a given.

She lowered herself to her knees, and I was regretting not choosing a redhead. But the brunette would do. She seemed hungry for it.

"Open your mouth and take it all," I instructed, not wanting the whole *eyeing me while she licked it like a lollipop* routine. It wasn't needed.

Her red-painted lips opened, and I thrust inside until I hit the back of her throat, grabbing a handful of her hair while doing so. The sound of her choking on it caused me to swell to full length.

"Ah, yeah, baby," I encouraged. "That's a tight mouth."

She sucked down harder from my words, greedy to please me. I liked that. Tonight, I fucking needed it.

"You keep that up, and you're gonna get that pussy filled."

She let out a moan and squirmed. I could see her move her hand between her legs and began playing with her pussy in the mirror.

Damn, I wished her hair was red.

FIVE YEARS AGO

"Fuuuck, Songbird," I groaned as she spread her legs for me on the blanket I'd laid over the damp grass.

The moonlight made her even more angelic in appearance.

"Keep playing with it," I begged her as I stroked my cock.

"I want you to put it all the way in this time," she said softly.

I lifted my gaze to her face, and, goddamn, she was gorgeous. All sweet, innocent, and sexy as hell.

"You sure?" I asked. "You see how big my cock is? That pussy is fucking tight."

It had squeezed my head so hard the last time I slid in the tip that I'd almost shot my load right then.

"I know," she whispered. "But I'm ready."

She was going to kill me. I'd been trying to be good. Get my fill by eating her pussy, letting her rub her bare cunt on my dick until she got off. And she'd recently started sucking me. There was nothing more beautiful than this girl with my cock in her mouth. I had been ready to worship at her altar the first time she did it.

"It hurts. You know that?"

She nodded.

"I hate hurting you."

"Please, Kash. I want you inside me. Fully. I want to know how it feels to be connected like that. With you."

Sweet Jesus. I couldn't tell her no. I didn't want to hurt her, but I wanted to sink inside her and not leave. Brand her as mine. Inside and out.

She was already naked. That was my first goal every time I brought her out here.

"Lie back," I instructed.

Her eyes lit up, and she smiled. She slowly moved back to her elbows, then eased onto her back. With her knees still bent and legs open to me. She was making fast, small pants as she watched me take off my shirt and toss it, then remove my jeans and underwear completely.

"You're beautiful," she said reverently.

"Songbird, if you don't want me to come the minute I put my head in your cunt, then don't look at me like that."

Her brows drew together slightly. "Like what?"

I grinned as I lowered my head between her legs. "As if I'm a god and you're my willing sacrifice," I replied before pressing a kiss to her swollen clit.

Her hands went to the back of my head, and her hips bucked at the first stroke of my tongue. "AH!" she cried out.

I continued licking her folds as she made sexy noises and pulled my hair.

"I—oh—this isn't what I asked for." She struggled with her words.

"Mmm," I hummed against her. "I'm getting you ready."

"Oh!" she squeaked and rocked her hips as I lapped up the sweetness between her legs.

She was close when I stopped and moved my body up over hers. Those eyes of hers were wide with desire and trepidation. She was nervous, but she didn't want me to know it.

"You're sure?" I asked, hoping like fuck she didn't change her mind.

Just thinking about it had me leaking pre-cum; I was so hard.

She nodded and opened her legs wider.

Grabbing my erection, I took the tip and ran it from her hard bud down to the entrance that I knew was going to own me the same way she did. When I pressed inside, she sucked in a breath, and as much as I wanted to watch my cock stretch her open, tear into her virginity, I wanted to see her face more.

She was biting her lip hard, and I reached and pulled it free. I didn't want her abusing it. I was partial to her full lower lip.

"I'm gonna do it in one hard thrust. Get the pain over with fast, okay?" I told her.

She nodded, then said, "I love you."

With those words from her pretty mouth, I shoved inside, feeling the thin membrane and breaking through it as she cried out beneath me. The suction took my breath as her inner walls closed in on my cock.

"Fuuuck," I shouted, having never felt this kind of nirvana before.

Her nails clawed my back as she held on to me. I tried to be still, but when I moved, it was incredible. The need to fuck her into the goddamn ground and unload my cum into her until it was dripping down her legs, mixed with the blood from her broken hymen, was almost too strong to fight against.

"I need to pump," I warned her. "The tightest pussy," I hissed. "Goddamn, baby, I need to—"

"Do it," she breathed against my ear as I lowered my head to the curve of her neck, trying to stay in control.

The animal I had barely been holding on to was unleashed with those two words, and a growl tore out of me. I thrust into her like a crazed man as words fell from my lips, along with sounds I'd never heard before.

"OH! Kash!" she cried out, and I became even wilder.

Our eyes locked, and I knew then that I'd never want or love another woman in my life. She was it for me. My little Songbird.

ELEVEN
CRESSIDA

Present Day

How did text messages just disappear? Had I hallucinated it? Chewing on my thumbnail, I stared at the phone on the kitchen counter, keeping my distance from it. The thing made me nervous now that I knew it had been given to me by the Southern Mafia and they had tracking devices on it. I'd barely gotten any sleep last night, afraid—and possibly, down deep, if I was honest with myself, a little hopeful—that Kash would show up again in my bedroom. He hadn't. But the text that had come in at four this morning, then vanished moments after I read it, showed up. And I wasn't sure who it was from—Kash or one of them. It had been an unknown number and simply said:

Unknown: Meet me in the backyard at midnight.

I wanted it to be Kash and not just because I foolishly wanted to see him again, but because the alternative terrified me. Sure, Kash was the only one of the Southern Mafia I'd seen kill someone, but he was the only one I trusted not to hurt me. To protect him, they'd make me disappear if they thought I was a threat. I knew it because I'd been told those exact words by his oldest brother, Oz, four years ago.

If Oz had found out about Kash coming here, then he'd follow through on that threat. Maybe I needed to leave town. Coming back to Madison wasn't any safer for me than staying at my father's. I should have gone somewhere new. Not back here. I needed more time to save money though. If I could just have one full month here, possibly two, then I could leave Madison and start out in an apartment somewhere that was in better condition than the one I'd had before.

The phone lit up again, and I froze. I'd silenced it this morning when I read the text. While I was with Glenda, I had no real reason for it. Panic seized me, making it hard for me to take a full breath. My gaze swung to the door that led to the sunroom, where Glenda was enjoying her breakfast, then back to the phone.

Cautiously, as if the phone itself could hurt me, I moved closer to it and winced as I leaned in to read the name on the screen. Another text. An unknown number.

Crap.

Crossing my arms over my chest, I stepped away. I didn't want to know what it said. Maybe ignorance was better.

No. I had been brave enough to run from Arthur. I could face this. Just another monster in my path. I'd been dealing with those since Pirate had hit puberty and morphed into one.

Straightening my shoulders, I took a deep breath and let it out slowly, then walked over and picked up the phone. Tapping the screen, I slid open the text.

> Unknown: Exit through the back door near the den. There are no cameras back there.

67

I read it twice before it was gone. Just like the one this morning. How was it doing that? I'd never known a text to be unsent after it had been read. Was that some new update?

I looked around the kitchen at the reminder of cameras that Kash was sure were in the house. Was I being watched now? Were they sending these to me and watching my reaction? Fear began to entwine with anger. It felt as if I was being toyed with for others' amusement. I didn't like that. Had I not suffered enough for these people?

I'd go out there tonight if that was what they wanted. I had done nothing wrong, and I was tired of constantly looking over my shoulder. I just wanted to be left alone to live my life. Find a place in this world where I fit. I wasn't here for Kash Savelle. And I'd tell whoever it was wanting me to meet them outside just that. Even if it was Kash himself.

Today was one of Glenda's busier days. I was thankful for that. There was little time to think about the texts this morning. Hurrying to check her post office box and pick up the list of items she needed from the grocery while she was in her yoga class, I pulled the coat I had found two days ago at a thrift store tighter around me and zipped it up. The breeze was biting today, and with the sudden drastic drop in temperature, I was glad I'd found one.

Glenda wanted to go do some Christmas shopping after her yoga class, and that left me with an hour and a half to accomplish my tasks. Just before I reached the door to the post office, I caught a glimpse of platinum-blonde hair. Glancing over that way, I froze at the sight of Saylor Rice, a man I didn't know with his arm around her waist, Gathe Bowen, and Kash. They were walking out of the popular breakfast spot in town. It had changed names in the past four years, but it looked the same. Saylor threw her head back and let out a musical laugh I remembered from high school. It was odd, seeing some other man touching her. Back then, she'd always been Crosby's.

Gathe was saying something that had them all smiling, and for a moment, I was back there. With them, at Kash's side. His arm around my shoulders. The scent of his leather and spice making me feel warm, safe, wanted.

His eyes locked on mine, as if he could read my thoughts from across the street, and his smile faded. I blinked, realizing the others might notice me too. They might all be beautiful, but they were the monsters. All of them a part of the family that everyone feared.

Turning, I shoved open the post office door and hurried inside. Out of the cold, away from their sight, I placed a hand on my heart as it raced in my chest. Whether it was from seeing Kash or the reaction to other Southern Mafia members, I wasn't sure. Both were threats, and until I could afford to leave this place, I had to be careful around them.

Glenda had one of the larger boxes, and it was at eye level for her convenience. I took out the key and unlocked it. Taking the tote bag I brought with me, I placed several envelopes, a few catalogs, and one box into the tote, then closed and locked it back up. No one else was around, so I stood there and waited. Giving Kash and the others time to leave. My heartbeat returned to normal as I stared at the clock on the wall, at the second hand ticking slowly. Once it had passed five minutes, I headed for the exit. They'd have made it to a vehicle by now and driven away.

I did a quick glance through the glass door, making sure they were out of sight before pushing it open and stepping back outside. The streets weren't empty; there were small shops, restaurants, and a bank with people rushing around. But there was no Southern Mafia around.

I headed back to Glenda's car, trying not to think about Kash Savelle.

"Cressida Beck."

I'd just started to open the car door when a female voice I'd not heard in years said my name. I recognized it, and dread sank over me. Ignoring the Mafia princess wasn't a good idea, so I turned around to face Saylor, expecting her to be with the others.

Except she was alone. Standing there, dressed like a runway model and looking like one in her long, shaggy fake fur coat and hot-pink boots, she smiled.

"It is you," she said. "I'll be damned."

It was likely she hadn't known about my return. Kash had told me once she wasn't let in on the inner workings. That her dad liked to keep her protected from the dark stuff.

"Hello, Saylor," I replied, unsure of what to say.

Her dimples appeared, making her all the more stunning. As if she needed any extra help in that department. "He knows you're in town, doesn't he?" she said. "His weird, distracted behavior all makes sense now."

He being Kash.

"I'm not here for him," I said quickly. "I am keeping my distance. Just working, saving money, so I can move on to somewhere else. I thought he was in Alabama when I came back here," I stammered out, hoping she would relay this to whoever needed to hear it.

Her eyebrows shot up. "I see. You're aware I don't care. If you've been spoken to by one of"—she smirked—"them, they don't tell me shit." She waved a hand. "Besides, he's only here for the holidays. Although it's obvious that he's seen you. I knew something was wrong with him."

I wanted to believe that, but with the family, I knew better than to trust anyone.

"Yes, he saw me on Tuesday. I was picking up laundry for my employer." *Stick with the truth they know.*

She scrunched her nose. "And earlier, when you were walking into the post office, he saw you then too."

I hesitated, then nodded.

She laughed softly as her eyes scanned the street, as if looking for someone. "That's why he left in a hurry," she murmured.

The man who'd had his arm around her earlier stepped out of the bookstore behind us and started in her direction. I glanced at him, then back at her. Just because I'd never met him did not mean he wasn't one of them. I doubted she'd be allowed to date outside the family.

"It was good to see you, but I need to go. I've got to get back to work," I told her.

The man slid his hand over her hip, and she tilted her head back to smile up at him. "Jude, this is Cressida Beck, an old friend of mine *and* Kash's," she said to him. "Cressida, this is Jude Rayne, my fiancé."

Great, she was introducing me. The fact that Rayne was not a last name I recognized was odd. Was he not in the Mafia? It didn't matter. Not my business. I needed to leave.

Jude held out a hand to me. "It's nice to meet you, Cressida," he said politely. No cocky swagger or darkness in his gaze.

I put my hand in his and shook it. "Same," I replied.

He appeared so … clean-cut and … proper even. Where had she found him? He was nothing like Crosby.

"It was good to see you again, Cressida," Saylor said.

I forced a smile, wishing I could say the same and mean it. Instead, I lied, "You too."

TWELVE

CRESSIDA

After a day of trying not to worry about it, I felt nauseous when I slowly opened the back door and stepped into the darkness. It was too dark. Where was the security light that was always on out here? I didn't move once I closed the door behind me. If I was walking out into the dark, I was going to do it once my eyes adjusted. I didn't know who it was that would be waiting out there, and I wanted to see them.

"Keep walking, Songbird," Kash's deep voice said in the blackness in front of me.

Relief came then, and the sick feeling eased. I wasn't about to be snatched up and shipped off—or worse. Kash might not like me, he might think I'd betrayed him, but he wasn't going to hurt me. At least not physically. I was certain of it.

I made my way down the stairs as I began to be able to make out more of the backyard with limited moonlight to help me. I didn't see Kash though. Which bothered me. Was he hiding?

"All the way back to the tree line," he said from the night, still unseen.

"Why?" I asked, not liking that idea.

"We can't be seen in the woods," he replied, sounding amused this time.

I didn't need to ask why he was worried about being seen.

I continued on and paused just outside the first row of trees and brush. It was too cold for bugs, but there could be other things that I didn't want to come in contact with. A hand wrapped around my wrist and tugged me, causing me to stumble forward and past the tree I was closest to. It was harder to see now with the moon blocked.

Kash's hands grabbed my waist and kept me from tripping over a tree root and falling on my face into God knew what. Once I was steady, I moved back, shoving his hands off me.

A deep chuckle sent a tingle through me that I mentally cursed.

"You got feisty," he said.

"What do you want, Kash?" I hissed.

He said nothing at first, and if I wasn't afraid he'd grab me again, I'd start back to the house.

"I don't know."

I frowned. He didn't know?

"You had me sneak out at midnight, walk blindly into the woods, and you don't know why?"

He stepped closer to me, and that scent of his that I used to love met my nose. I refused to inhale deeply.

"You didn't answer questions that I need answers to," he said.

"What questions?" I bit out, more angry at myself for my reaction to him than anything.

"Why aren't you working toward your dream of starting a theatre arts program for kids?"

73

He remembered. I'd almost forgotten it myself. When I'd had to give up my plans and goals to survive, I had tried to lock them away. Not torture myself with what I'd never have.

"Life sucks, Kash. And we move on," I replied bitterly.

"That's not an answer. The girl I knew was passionate about it. About life. Her future."

"The girl you knew died a long time ago. Along with all her fairy tales. If that is all you came here to ask, then I'm going back inside," I said, ready to run away from the memories, from him.

His reflexes were faster though, and his hand was locked around my arm before I could even turn to leave. "No, you're not. You've not answered shit."

"Why do you care?!" I demanded, angry that he was making me think about it all.

He leaned close to me, and I stilled.

"Because even though I want to hate you or just not fucking care, it seems I do. Now, tell me why you're here. What happened to you the past four years?"

I tried to jerk free, already knowing he was stronger than me. "What happened to you?!" I shot back at him.

He wanted me to talk, yet he wasn't telling me anything.

He moved closer, and I backed up, but almost immediately was stopped by a tree. My back pressed against the bark of the trunk, and I glared up at him. Dammit, even in the blanket of darkness, his blue eyes stood out.

"You want to know?" His tone turned threatening, and I stiffened. "I live in a state I don't particularly like. I work beside guys who aren't my family. I've been homesick. Miss my life here. Everything I lost. Because of you. My obsession with you ..." He lowered his face until I could feel his breath on my cheek. He smelled of mint and whiskey. "You took it all from me. Even my goddamn soul ..." He paused and let out a low hissing sound. "And even then, I want to rip your pants off and fuck you against this tree like the animal you always seemed to bring out in me."

Tears burned my eyes, and I was thankful now for the dark shadows. Maybe he wouldn't see. I sucked in a breath and swallowed hard. Too many emotions were unleashed by his words. Painful, brutal, and tempting words. The temptation to beg him to do it. Take me. Remind me what it felt like to be his was there. Entirely too close to the surface.

"Your turn, Songbird," he said harshly. "Tell me about the last four years."

Thinking clearly with him this close was a challenge. My brain was telling me to beat on his chest and tell him to let me go. My body, on the other hand, wanted to rub up against him like a cat. Neither wanted to talk about my past.

He ran a callous finger down my cheek, stopping at my chin. "I'm waiting."

I inhaled sharply. Fine. He wanted to know. He had laid his false accusations out. What he believed had happened the night he killed Pirate. He'd not given me a chance to explain. He'd left me shattered.

"We left town because my mother couldn't take the scandal of Pirate's death. She went into deep depression and was put on meds for it. She also started drinking heavily," I said through the lump forming in my throat. I hated talking about it. The image of her under the water. The horror of what I'd found. "One morning, I went to wake her up. She always slept late due to drinking on the meds, and it was getting closer to noon. I was worried." I paused and closed my eyes. "She wasn't in her bed. It was still made up. I-I went looking for her. Checked every room to see if she'd passed out somewhere else that night. When she wasn't in the house, I went outside." I stopped, shaking my head. I didn't want to tell him more. I didn't want to say it.

"You said she drowned." His voice wasn't angry anymore. "Did you find her?" he asked with a trace of pain, making it easier to nod my head. "Jesus," he muttered.

Needing to get it out, finish so he'd let me go, I blurted out the rest. "My dad married his secretary six months later. She was almost twenty years younger than him, and she didn't like me, but it wasn't until they were married that I realized it. She had a younger brother, Arthur." My voice cracked as I said his name. "He helped me deal with her. We ... I thought we were friends. We went to the movies together; he took me to New York to see musicals on Broadway. And at first, it was nice. Not being alone. But he changed. He became possessive and controlling. It ... it got to the point where I didn't feel safe. So, I left. No, I ran."

I took a deep, ragged breath and finally lifted my eyes from his chest to meet his eyes again. There. I'd told him what he wanted to know.

"Did he touch you? Hurt you?" Kash asked through clenched teeth.

The savage glint in his eyes I'd only seen one other time. The night he'd killed Pirate. I didn't want to lie to him, but I also didn't trust his reaction to the truth. I remained silent.

"Cressida," he demanded. His hand gripped my chin, firmly holding my head so I couldn't look away from him. "Did he hurt you?"

Yes. Many times. It was why I'd run. Why I'd had no other choice.

"I'm not your problem anymore, Kash," I reminded him.

His eyes dropped to my mouth, and I stopped breathing. A war of what I wanted and what I feared battling in my head.

76

"You shouldn't be," he said, lifting his gaze back to mine. "I wish like hell you weren't. That I didn't care. But you didn't give me back my soul when you ripped it to shreds." His nostrils flared. "Did. He. Hurt. You?"

Lie. Lie, Cressida. Lie to save a life. One that might not deserve it. Lie to save yourself future pain because it will come with a price.

The world balanced things out, and I already knew that being saved by Kash, in the way he handled things, only sent the bad karma my way.

"Your silence is my answer," he said. "Don't admit it. I can read it in your eyes, Songbird." He released my chin and stepped back.

"No! He didn't hurt me physically," I lied, moving toward him, as if I could grab him and stop him. "It was just emotional."

His hands fisted at his sides as his chest rose and fell with heavy breathing. "I don't care," he snarled, and I backed up.

He stalked back toward me, planting a hand on either side of my head, caging me against the tree. His eyes were wild, and I thought maybe I had been wrong. Perhaps I should be scared of him.

"I fucked a stripper last night," he said more calmly, although his eyes didn't change.

I winced. Why would he tell me that?

"I let her suck me, then bent her over a bar and fucked her hard. Pounded into her wet cunt like a man possessed."

I closed my eyes, wishing I could unhear this. Images I didn't want in my head. The pain that came with it was unbearable, and I hated that, after all this time, he affected me this way. That I cared.

His hot breath was on my neck, and I stiffened. "And when I shot my load into the condom," he said in my ear, "it was your name I shouted. Yours. And it wasn't the first time I'd done it."

Oh God. My eyes opened to see him run a finger along my neck as he studied it.

"I came so hard, thinking about you," he whispered. "I always do."

Why was this turning me on? What was wrong with me? The tingle between my legs meant I was as deranged as him, apparently. I was struggling to breathe.

His gaze moved up my neck, pausing at my mouth before meeting my eyes.

"Did that make you wet, little Songbird?"

I shook my head. I wasn't admitting that.

A wicked smirk curled his lips. "Liar."

I shook my head again, but when he shoved his hand down the front of my leggings, my knees buckled, and a cry escaped me. His long middle finger slid between my folds easily as he grabbed my waist and held me up. A dark, pleased laugh came from him.

"I stand corrected. Not wet. Soaked."

I closed my eyes, unable to look at him. He was right. I was a terrible person.

His finger met my entrance, and he thrust it inside me.

"AH!" I screamed and grabbed his arms.

"Jesus Christ, how is it still so tight?" His words sounded like a groan.

I rocked against his hand, no longer worried about anything more than this moment.

"Needy cunt," he said, leaning in so close that his nose brushed mine. "Sucking my finger so greedily."

I'd forgotten about his dirty talk … no, I hadn't, but I'd forgotten how much it affected me.

I moaned from the pleasure I'd not had in so long.

"You're gonna get my dick if you keep this up," he warned. The excitement in his tone just made me move faster.

"Fuck!" he swore, pulling his hand from me.

I opened my eyes, panicked that he was stopping, only to see him jerking down his jeans and pulling out his cock. A small square package he must have taken from his pocket was torn open, and he rolled the condom down over his erection. He took a step toward me and then grabbed the waist of my leggings and jerked them down, along with my panties. He only pulled out one leg, then stood up and hiked my free leg up to his waist, not pausing before slamming into me.

"OH GOD!" I shouted out as an animalistic sound came from him.

As he started thrusting into me, he slid a hand behind my back to keep my skin from hitting the rough bark and squeezed my butt hard in the process.

"Is this what you wanted, Songbird?" he asked. "My cock taking your hot little cunt."

I was past lying. I nodded, feeling frantic. My memories hadn't done this justice. The way he filled me, how having his hard body slapping against mine was its own erotic song.

"You're so goddamn wet; it's running down my balls," he said as he bit my neck the licked it. "I missed this. Sweet body taking me."

I was already there. I felt the crest just about to hit, and my nails sank into his back.

"KASH!" I cried out as the rush of ecstasy hit me.

"Fu-uck," he groaned. "That's it; come on my cock. Fuck, baby, GAH!" He threw his head back and let out a roar as his body jerked against mine.

The sight he made only sent me over the edge once more.

THIRTEEN

CRESSIDA

The chill in the air returned, even with my skin flushed, when Kash slid out of me and jerked up his pants, stepping away as if I'd bitten him. Suddenly aware of my almost-naked body, I scrambled to get my leg back in my leggings and pulled them back up, not bothering to straighten my panties. Once I was covered, I wrapped my arms around my body and looked into the darkness, where he stood. I had felt connected to him again only moments before, but clearly, it hadn't been the same for him. I was foolish for having thought what we had done meant something.

"Maybe now we can have our closure." Kash's voice was low and void of any emotion.

"Closure?" I asked in disbelief. Was that truly what that had been for him?

"Yeah. We both needed it. Time to move on and put the past behind us. We're different people now."

And with that, he turned and began walking away. Leaving me there in the night alone. Not even watching me walk back to the house. He just left.

FOUR YEARS AGO

I gripped the covers tightly, watching in horror as my door handle rattled gently. I'd locked it, but the sound told me it was being picked. I should have put a chair under the door handle too. But if Kash had shown up at my window and seen that, he'd want to know why I had myself barricaded in my bedroom. Or maybe he wouldn't ask. He'd know.

Lately, Pirate had started getting braver around him. Showing glimpses of his twisted mind. Kash was suspicious. He didn't trust him and had already asked me several times if Pirate bothered me at home.

Telling him the truth wasn't something I could do. This was my own demon to fight, and so far, I'd handled it. But Pirate was making it harder.

Easing out of the bed, I walked over to the baseball bat I had placed there last week. I'd gone looking for it in the attic and brought it down to my room as a means of protection if needed. Stepping back farther away from the door, I waited with it, held at the ready.

Pirate had stopped being my brother, someone I trusted. His sick mind and unstable behavior made him a threat. I was relieved when he left for college, but that was short-lived. He came home every weekend, and by the end of the first semester, he'd failed every course. Our parents refused to pay for him to continue, and he moved back home. He was seeing a therapist, per my mother's requirements for him living here, but it didn't seem to be helping.

If I could just get through this semester, I was going to move on campus. If he was staying here, I had to get out. My choice to not live on campus was to save my parents some money, but I'd get a student loan if I needed to. I had already started reading up on how to do that.

The lock clicked, and a cold dread settled over me. I braced both my feet and kept my gaze locked on the door. It opened slowly, and then Pirate stepped into the room, his focus on my empty bed. When he realized I wasn't in it, his gaze narrowed and scanned the room until it landed on me.

The evil smirk on his lips made me shiver. I hated him. I'd felt guilty for that once, but he'd made it so that I no longer did. He'd caused this. He'd ruined any relationship we'd once had. The first night, I'd woken up to find him in my bed and his hand inside my panties. I'd thrown up several times that night. Sick from what he had done to me.

"A bat, Cressida?" he asked, amused, as he closed the door behind him.

"Yes, and if you come close enough, I will slam it against your head," I warned him.

There was no fear or concern in his eyes, but they were black. His dilated pupils giving away the fact he was high. Something I doubted he shared with his therapist. His addiction to narcotics.

"You won't do anything to upset your mom." He slurred his words as he began walking toward me.

He never referred to our parents as his. From the first day in this house, he had been full of anger. I knew Mom thought that they could provide the emotional support and love he needed to fix him, but Pirate had been broken beyond repair a very long time ago.

I pulled the bat back, ready to swing, and that finally got him to pause. I thought it was because of fear that I would hit him, but his eyes shot to the window behind me.

"Motherfucker," he muttered with disgust, but he paled slightly and began to back away. "You tell him anything, and I'll kill your mother in her sleep," he warned before leaving my room much quicker than he'd entered it.

I heard it then, the slight scratch of Kash climbing the tree outside my bedroom window. I rushed to the bed and shoved the bat under it, not wanting him to see it, then hurried back to the window just as he reached me.

If he only knew how many nights he'd saved me from Pirate, showing up like this. Kash Savelle was my own personal hero in a sexy, bad-boy package.

PRESENT DAY

Shivering under the covers, I stared into the darkness as the tears wet my pillow. It wasn't the first time I'd cried myself to sleep over Kash Savelle, but it had been years. The wound that had been poorly bandaged on my heart was ripped open once again, and the hollowness was an aching void I had no way to fill. I'd survived without him before, and I knew I could do it again. But first, I needed to let the pain out. Mourn for all that was lost. The love that I feared I'd never know again.

FOURTEEN
CRESSIDA

If Glenda noticed the dark circles under my eyes that I had done my best to cover with concealer, she didn't mention it. I was thankful she hadn't asked me if I was okay because, honestly, I was afraid I'd burst into tears if she did. The heaviness in my chest wasn't easing as the day went on, and last night kept replaying in my head.

The doorbell caught me off guard since people rarely stopped by that Glenda wasn't expecting. Actually, other than some Jehovah's Witnesses last week, it had never happened.

"Lordy be," Glenda called out from the sunroom. "I wonder who is stopping by for a visit. Could you get that, Cressida? I need to go put on something other than my nightgown and housecoat."

"Yes," I replied, already heading toward the door.

It could possibly be someone raising money for the less fortunate. That was common this time of year. If so, I was going to go get some of my savings I had tucked away. Thoughts of Burt came to mind, and I felt guilty for not going to check on him. While I was living in warmth and a comfortable bed, he was out in the cold and hungry.

With my thoughts on Burt, I opened the door without checking the window beside it to see who it was. The sight of Bane Cash standing there sent a jolt of fear through me. I'd not seen him in years. He was older and even more intimidating in appearance than I remembered. The man had a scowl that sent shivers down my spine.

Frozen, I stared at him. It took a moment for it to register in my head that Glenda was his great-aunt. He wasn't here for me. At least, I didn't think so.

Had there been a camera that caught me going outside to meet Kash last night after all?

"Is Glenda home?" he asked.

I swallowed, then nodded and forced myself to take a step back so that he could come inside. His large presence filled the doorway, and I held my breath as he passed me.

Kash had shared many things about the family with me back when we were together. Like the fact that, one day, Bane would be the head of the Mississippi branch. He was also lethal and the most dangerous out of all of them.

"Is she in her sunroom?" His tone wasn't sharp, but more cold.

Had he been the one to place me here under their watch? His mother had come to find me. Maybe he was the head now. I didn't know anything about them anymore.

"N-no," I stammered. "She's getting dressed. Y-you can wait in the sunroom for her if you'd like." My heart was pounding so hard that I feared he might hear it.

He turned then and leveled his glare on me. "I told you that you'd only get one warning." His voice was low and deep.

Oh God. He knew.

I shook my head. "I didn't—he came …" I paused because what if he didn't know and I was about to blurt it out?

"You can leave town, or I'll escort you out."

Leave town? Where would I go? I barely had enough to rent another apartment. I needed more time.

"I-I-I would leave now if I could," I began as my entire body trembled. "I don't want to see him. I wanted to start a new life. But I don't have the money yet. I just need some more time."

His jaw worked as he studied me.

I was past the tremble and now visibly shaking. This felt like a panic attack building.

"When he came, you went to him," he said between clenched teeth.

He knew.

"I will never make that mistake again," I swore, and I meant it.

Kash had hurt me for the last time. I couldn't survive it again. I was barely hanging on as it was.

"Pack your things. I'll handle things with my aunt. Tomorrow night, I will pick you up at ten. She doesn't need any goodbyes from you. Don't speak of this to her," he said. "And if you say anything to Kash, I will know. You're leaving won't go nearly as smoothly as it will if you keep quiet."

He was taking me? Where? Smoothly? My throat was so tight that I couldn't breathe.

"You're white. Don't pass the fuck out. I'm giving you what you want. A new start away from here. I'm not going to kill you."

I sucked in a full breath, then let out a small sob of relief and disbelief. Tears burned my eyes, and I wasn't sure if I could keep from crying.

"Go get yourself under control. I don't want Glenda seeing you like this. She'll blame me," he ordered harshly and pointed toward the hallway.

I nodded and bolted past him as quickly as I could without running. Just as I reached my door, I heard Glenda turning the knob on hers, and I slipped inside my temporary room as quietly as I could.

"Cressida, dear, who was it?" she called out, and I stayed silent.

"It's me, Aunt Glenda," Bane replied.

"Oh! Bane, what a lovely surprise!" she said, sounding thrilled to have him visit.

"I felt a visit was overdue," he told her as I sank against the door.

"It is! But where is my boy?!"

Bane chuckled, and the sound was almost pleasant. I frowned, thinking how odd it seemed, coming from him.

"He has a dentist appointment this morning. Mom wanted to go with Halo and him, so I thought I'd come see you instead."

Bane Cash had a kid? Was that what I was hearing? How very … terrifying. A man like him should not have children. What female was brave enough to get near him? Sure, he was attractive. I wasn't blind, but he was also Satan with none of the charm that his brother had possessed.

I closed my eyes and took a deep breath. Okay, this was not important. I had to focus. Bane had said he was giving me what I wanted. Which was? Leaving and starting a new life? I'd told him I didn't have the money for that.

"Cressida?" Glenda called my name, and I straightened, then turned to take the doorknob.

"I believe she needed to use the ladies' room," Bane told her. "Why don't we go have a seat in the sunroom? Catch me up on all your activities."

He didn't want me out there. I waited as their voices faded while they walked away.

I didn't have a choice. Bane would come for me, and I'd have to leave. The small amount of security I'd found here was being taken from me. All because I'd been unable to stay away from Kash. Once again, my need for him had cost me the sliver of stability I'd had. But then had it really been stable? I'd been under the control of the Southern Mafia the entire time.

I should have never come back here.

FIFTEEN
KASH

Four Years Ago

Something had been off lately with Cressida. She assured me she was fine, but she was lying. Her eyes gave her away. They always had. It was one of the things I loved about her.

She had fallen asleep while we were texting. She did that often. It was cute, but tonight, I wasn't able to relax. Sleep wasn't coming, and my gut had me getting in my truck and driving to her house. I normally didn't come this late, even when I was sneaking in her window. It would most likely scare her if I woke her up, but I needed to see she was okay.

If she would just move in with me, then this wouldn't be an issue. But she said it would upset her parents, and they'd likely stop paying her tuition. I'd told her I'd pay it. I wanted to be the one taking care of her anyway. But she didn't want the drama and fallout. I was trying to be patient with her, but I was getting real damn close to proposing. We were young, but if it was going to take marriage to get her to let me take care of her, then we'd go ahead and do it. She was my end-game anyway.

Parking my truck down the street near the park, I headed out on foot to her house at a jog. The closer I got, the more anxious I felt. I'd wanted to hear her voice tonight, but she had said she couldn't talk on the phone because her mother was still up and working in the guest bedroom across the hall. She'd been turning it into a craft room for over a month now. When was she going to be fucking finished with it?!

All the lights in the house were off, including the craft room. No one was awake, but I'd assumed as much. It was almost three.

Using all the stealth that came with my training, which had started at puberty, I made my way up the tree. The window was cracked, and I smirked. She never fully closed or locked it at night, just in case I stopped by. Reaching over, I slid it up slowly and squinted into the darkness. Slipping inside, I left it up in case I needed to escape quickly. Her parents had never woken up before though. They both took sleeping meds. If they didn't, I'd have drugged their wine bottles. Luckily, they made it easy for me.

I'd not taken the first step when I saw it. The other figure in the bed. I blinked, unsure I was seeing it clearly, although the blood I heard rushing in my ears told me I was. For a moment, I didn't move. I stood there and stared at them. My world hadn't just tilted from its axis, but it had been taken and fucking thrown against a wall, exploding into pieces.

Pain became a monster as it roared through me. I bent over, grabbing my knees as I tried to breathe through the crushing weight on my chest.

My Songbird. My goddamn soul. How could she do this?

Every inhale felt like my lungs were on fire. My temples pounded, and a beast began to unravel. The fury unfolding wasn't normal anger. It wanted blood. The image of Pirate lying beside her, his arm around her as they slept, was burned into my memory. Even if I wasn't looking at them, I'd never be able to unsee it.

Had he fucked her?

My head snapped up, and I began moving. Long strides, I was no longer in control. The agony that had morphed into bloodlust and madness had taken over. It was as if I was on the outside, looking at this from afar. Or perhaps that was my sanity. I'd left it on the floor the moment I saw them together like that.

When I was standing over him, I began to picture all I would do. Slice off his hand first. Then his limp dick. I'd shove it in his mouth and let him gag on it while I continued cutting him up, piece by piece.

The betrayal clawed at me like a wild animal. It felt as if it was ripping my skin over and over.

She moved, turning, and her lashes fluttered as she began to wake before she stilled, then shot out of bed as if it were on fire. Her wide eyes went from Pirate in her bed to me standing over him. My knife already in my hand. Even now, after finding her like this, the urge to protect her coursed through me, trying to overpower the other. She was MINE! Yet she'd let another touch her.

"Did you fuck him?" I seethed.

She began shaking her head frantically. "No! No! I—"

"What the—" Pirate cut her off as his eyes opened, and he stared up at me. My knife at his throat silenced him.

The fear in his eyes should give me some pleasure, but I would feel none. She'd robbed me of ever feeling any pleasure again.

"Kash, don't—" she began to plead.

"If you beg for his life, it will be more brutal," I warned her.

Tears filled her eyes, and she trembled. Did she love him? Her gaze dropped to his, and when his locked with hers, my grip on the blade in my hand tightened, and I shoved it through his ribs and pierced his lung. The moment it sank inside the organ, I let out a savage growl. His breathing instantly became fast and short. I thrust harder. I heard Cressida say my name, I heard her crying, but for once, I didn't care. She would watch him die. Right here in the room she'd betrayed me in.

PRESENT DAY

"Where were you last night?"

I hadn't heard Oz enter the kitchen, but then I hadn't even known he was here. I stood, staring at the espresso machine as it filled my cup. I'd not fallen asleep last night. My inability to take a goddamn shower and wash her scent from my body probably didn't help.

"Where were you?" I shot back at him.

He let out a heavy sigh. "Why can't you stay the fuck away from her?" he asked in a whispered growl.

Fuck. He knew I'd gone to see Cressida. That meant Bane most likely knew too. Dammit!

"I don't see anything wrong with visiting an old friend," I replied, taking my cup, then turning to look at him.

Oz ran a hand through his hair, frustration marring his brow. "Because you are a fucking psycho when it comes to that girl."

I shrugged, trying not to show him how close to the truth he was. "I was a kid. I'm not that kid anymore. I was curious as to how her life had turned out and why she was at Aunt Glenda's, working as a sitter. I don't see any issue with it. No one has to know. I got my answers, and I don't plan on seeing her again."

I'd also kept the used condom because it smelled like her cunt. Yeah, not psycho at all.

"She's not good for you. Seeing her isn't good for your mental health. You were toxic together. Where she was concerned, you were insane. You stabbed her goddamn brother in her bed and watched him bleed to death."

I took a drink before responding, "Thanks for the recap. I was there. I've also stabbed other men and watched them bleed to death. We all have."

Oz shook his head. "Not the same thing, and you know it."

"True. I didn't cut him in pieces and toss him to the hogs."

"Fuck, Kash. Don't you want to come home? Stay?"

I nodded. "More than anything."

"Then act like it!"

Did that mean I had a chance at getting to stay? Cressida's face last night when she'd come with my cock buried deep inside her flashed in my head. I'd be near her. Could I stay away from her? I'd spouted some shit about closure last night and let her think I'd left so that I could calm down. Get my head on straight. Watching her wipe tears from her cheeks as she walked into that house alone about broke me. But it had to be done. My staking a claim on her and carrying her off like a caveman wasn't an option.

I had stood out there in the woods, watching her window well past the time her lamp turned off. The sun was threatening to rise when I finally walked back to my Hummer. I'd typed out and deleted at least ten text messages to her.

"I will. I am. Like I said, just went to talk to her. See how she was doing. Nothing more."

He said nothing as he studied me for any sign of a lie. He wasn't going to get one. I took another drink.

"Is that all? Can I go get a shower now?" I asked him sarcastically.

Hopefully, he left and didn't hang around because I wasn't taking a shower. Not while her scent clung to my skin.

"You promise me you'll stay away from her?" he asked.

"Scout's honor."

"Funny," he drawled.

I smirked and walked past him. He needed to leave so I could decide just how I was going to kill this brother of her stepmother's once I found out who he was and where he lived.

SIXTEEN
CRESSIDA

If I'd been asleep, I wouldn't have heard it. The smallest creak of the floorboard outside the bedroom door. Wiping at my tears, I sat up, clutching the covers to my chest, and stared at the closed door. Nothing happened. Had I imagined it?

The doorknob turned then, and I held my breath. I knew without seeing him who it was. Kash had texted me again today. Told me to meet him outside at midnight. I hadn't. I went to bed, only to lie here and cry. Midnight had come and gone. It was almost one thirty.

His tall, dark form slipped inside the room, and the door quietly closed behind him. The moonlight spilling in from the windows illuminated his face, and I hoped it didn't shine on mine. I didn't have to see myself to know my eyes were red and swollen.

"You need to leave," I said in a hoarse whisper. "We had our closure," I reminded him.

His long, muscular legs took only a few strides before he was there beside my bed. I didn't want to make eye contact or turn so he could see my face, but he grabbed my chin roughly and forced it. He leaned down close to me, his gaze almost menacing.

"What? Did you think a fuck in the woods meant I forgave you?" he sneered. "You shredded me, my soul. Your betrayal didn't just ruin my life; it ruined me. Destroyed me." He leaned in closer, and I tried to pull my chin from his hold, but it tightened, and he held me there. "Yeah, Songbird, I fucked you. But my cock doesn't seem to hold a grudge." He let me go then with a shove that jerked my head to the side.

I was torn between anger and sorrow. Closing my eyes, I fought off the onset of more tears. They accomplished nothing and only made me appear guilty and weak. I was neither.

"Then leave," I croaked.

"I wish like fuck I could. I wish the scent of you on my skin wasn't so damn addictive that I can't make myself take a shower."

I pressed my lips together to hold in a sob, then took a steady breath.

"You hate me for something you think I did," I said in a hoarse whisper. "But you never asked me. Never let me explain."

"I saw it!" he hissed through his teeth, interrupting me. "I didn't need a motherfucking detailed description or a lie!"

I didn't know if it was the false accusation, his lack of faith in me, or simply four years of pain that caused it, but I snapped.

I jerked my head back around to face him, and my hands fisted in my lap as I dropped the covers. "But you're here," I said with more force. "So, you can listen or leave."

He made no move to go anywhere, so I began to purge the truth I'd never been able to share.

"Pirate broke into my bedroom that night and got into my bed while I was sleeping. I had known he could pick the lock, so I'd started adding a chair beneath the doorknob for added protection. But that night, while my mom worked in the room across from me, I'd been afraid to barricade the door while she was awake in case she tried to come in, and I fell asleep, texting with you, before she went to bed. When I woke up, I realized he was in my bed and panicked, and then I saw you with the knife." I stopped and swallowed. "And I was relieved. I knew you would kill him, and I was relieved. Not thinking past what that meant for either of us. Just that I wouldn't have to live in fear in my own house anymore." I sucked in a breath.

I'd never admitted it out loud. My desire for Pirate to die. But it was true. He'd made me a monster too. One who wished death on another.

"Why did you know he would pick your lock?" The question was one I'd expected.

"That was my lie of omission. Something I kept from you to protect you because if you knew, you'd do exactly what you did, and I was scared of what would happen to you if you did."

His nostrils flared, and his eyes narrowed. "What did you protect me from, Cressida?"

"Six months after we started dating, I woke up to Pirate in bed with me and his hand down the front of my panties." I winced from the bile in my throat. "I screamed. He covered my mouth and held me there. He told me if I ever said anything to anyone, he'd kill Mom in her sleep. We heard the footsteps on the stairs then, and he hurried out of my room. When my mom got to my room to see why I had screamed, I told her it was a nightmare."

Kash's chest was rising and falling as he took hard, fast breaths. He shoved a hand through his black hair and fisted it, then began to pace.

I sat, saying no more as I watched him.

"You should have told me that night. Called me. He'd have been gone before morning," Kash said, shaking his head as if he were a caged animal.

"I thought I was protecting y—"

He moved so fast that I almost let out a yelp, but he was in my face before I could utter a sound. "I protect you! Me. I'm the protector. You're mine to protect." His words went from rage to desperation. He placed both his palms on the mattress beside me and hung his head, letting out a ragged breath. "You *were* mine to protect. And I failed."

A tear rolled down my face, and I shook my head even though he wasn't looking at me. "No. You stopped him. I might have lost you, but you ended the nightmare."

He let out a laugh. It wasn't amused or hard but filled with pain. When he lifted his head and leveled his eyes on me, I let out a sob. The unsaid words, anguish for all that was no more, it was there in his blue eyes.

"I still failed you," he said in a husky voice. "And I can't undo it. I have to live with it."

"We were young. Pirate was not well. I'm equally to blame," I told him, hating the raw vulnerability in his eyes as they turned glassy.

I couldn't stand seeing him like this. Kash was unbreakable. He was fierce, wild, dangerous. If he cried, I would fall apart.

He clenched his jaw as he fought for control over the onslaught of emotions we were both dealing with.

"Can I hold you?" he asked.

I nodded and moved over so that he could sit down on the bed. Once he was seated with his back against the headboard and his feet stretched out in front of him and crossed at the ankles, he reached over and pulled me to his chest with his arm around my shoulders.

I didn't hesitate and went willingly, burying my face in his chest, then began to sob.

When I opened my eyes, the sunlight filled the room, and I was alone with the only reassurance that Kash had ever been there was the smell of leather and spice on the pillow he'd leaned against.

SEVENTEEN
KASH

"You gonna tell us why we're going to Arkansas?" Gathe asked, staring at me like I'd lost my mind over his mug of beer.

"I need to find a man named Arthur Howt," I told him.

"Then do what with him?" Than asked.

"Kill him," I replied.

He sighed and leaned back in his chair. "Damn. I was afraid that was the answer."

"Tell me this has nothing to do with Cressida," Gathe said with dread.

"Of course it does," Than said, picking up his glass. "If Kash is going to kill a man without an order, it's about Cressida."

Gathe set his mug down and placed his elbows on the table as he leaned in my direction. "You are aware that it is mentally unstable for you to off every man she's fucked?"

"She didn't fuck him," I said, hating to even think about her with another man.

"He's got the wild look in his eyes," Than said. "I'd back up."

Gathe straightened while studying me. "You do this, and they'll find out. Then there is no way in hell you'll get to move home."

"He's right," Than added. "Is it really worth it? What did the man do?"

I picked up my whiskey glass and downed it, needing something to take the edge off as I thought about the things Cressida had and hadn't told me. "Enough. He hurt her. His sister is her stepmother."

Than winced. "I didn't know she had one of those."

"Her mom is dead."

"Damn," Gathe muttered. "I mean, when you say *hurt*, like how exactly? Hurt her feelings? Grabbed her? We gotta weigh this against you being banished to Alabama for life."

I didn't know exactly, but I would. When I had him strung up, I'd get him to talk. "It's worth it. I'm going with or without you. It'll be easier with help, but I can do it alone."

Than blew out another long breath. "Fine. If we can't stop you, I'm not letting you go alone."

Gathe turned to look at Than. "I'm not letting him go alone either, but you coulda tried harder to change his mind about this before you caved."

Than rolled his eyes. "He's only been gone for four years. Have you forgotten that he's a stubborn motherfucker? We would be wasting our breath. It has to do with Cressida."

"We need to leave tonight. Bane is leaving. Not sure where, but I overheard Oz telling Dad that Bane had some business to handle and was going out of town tonight. Linc doesn't seem to be the one who doesn't trust me. Bane, however, has sent a threatening text to Cressida to stay away from me."

Gathe scrunched his nose. "How did she know it was Bane? Mighta been Linc. Sounds like him."

"It was Bane's number. He didn't even block it from her when he texted."

"And you know this how?" Gathe asked.

"He's in contact with her, most likely been to see her. How else does he know about Arthur?" Than said with annoyance.

Gathe nodded. "Oh, yeah. Makes sense."

"And she's working for Aunt Glenda," I told them both.

Than's eyes widened slightly. "No shit?"

I nodded.

"If Bane is gonna be this fucking controlling, why doesn't he take over already?" Gathe asked, taking another drink.

"I don't think he wants to," Than said with a shrug.

"We leave at eight," I told them, not giving a shit about the other.

"Do we even have an address?" Gathe asked as I stood up.

I cut my eyes at him.

He held up his hands. "Fine. You got an address. I was just asking."

"I've got every address of every person directly and indirectly connected with him."

Than chuckled.

"What's his shoe size?" Gathe asked, smirking.

"Ten and a half," I replied. "And he has narrow feet."

Than was still laughing as I made my way to the front door of the Bowens' house. Once I'd had a first and last name, I'd been able to do a complete background check on the bastard. Unlike Cressida, his hadn't been locked away or wiped clean.

EIGHTEEN

CRESSIDA

Bane had not spoken a word to me since I'd walked out of Glenda's house, other than holding out his hand and saying, "Phone."

I'd placed the cell phone, given to me by his mother, in it, knowing that was my only connection to Kash.

He'd not texted me today. I'd not gotten to say goodbye. Did he even know I was leaving? I had so many questions and no one to ask.

After last night, it felt like everything had changed. I'd fallen asleep with the first stirring of hope for … us.

But the Southern Mafia wanted me out of Kash's life, and that left me no other choice. I had to go.

We'd driven to a private airstrip, boarded a plane, and he slept during the hour flight. I couldn't close my eyes. We hit turbulence more than once, and the landing was rough, but he only opened his eyes once the wheels touched the ground. I'd expected him to say something, but he didn't.

I wanted to ask where we were, but I was also terrified of the man. It wasn't until the black Escalade, which picked us up when we got off the plane, passed under a sign on the interstate that said something about Orlando that I knew he'd brought me to Florida.

I looked around, hoping he wasn't leaving me in Orlando because that was going to be too expensive. I was pretty sure all of Florida was going to be too expensive. Why hadn't he chosen a cheaper state? I didn't have enough money for this, and if he left me here, I had no car. I'd have to buy a bus ticket.

Clearing my throat so my voice wouldn't crack when I spoke, I straightened my shoulders and tried not to look nervous. "Are you leaving me here, in Florida?" I asked him.

He cut his eyes at me and nodded, then went back to watching out the window. I thought that was going to be the only response I got, but he finally spoke.

"Ocala, to be exact," he said.

"Do I have to stay here? Like I told you, I don't have much money, and this state isn't an affordable one."

"I told you that I was giving you what you wanted. A new life. A place to start over. I don't do things half-assed, and I'd like to be sure you stay away from Mississippi and Kash," he said, then briefly glanced at me again. "Your apartment is fully furnished. Rent and utilities have been paid for six months. There is a car in the parking lot, and the key fob will be on your kitchen counter. Information on your job, where to be and when, is also on your kitchen counter."

I opened my mouth, then closed it twice. Then I just gaped at him.

He turned his cold gaze to me again. "You have all you need to start a new life. Do it and stay the fuck away from Mississippi."

I hesitated before I blurted, "You're serious?"

He cocked an eyebrow. "Why would I lie about this?"

I shook my head still reeling. "I … I … but why? I mean, I don't understand."

"You don't?" he asked with an air of sarcasm. "Let me clear it up for you. It's time Kash comes home to stay. He belongs in Madison. But he can't stay there if you are there. It's a dangerous distraction. You make him act irrationally. I'd have thought you'd understand that. Do you want him killing every man you decide to fuck?"

I paled.

"What? The reminder that he caught you in bed with your brother hard for you to hear?" The snarl in his tone made my stomach twist.

"I … I didn't do anything with him, Pirate. I didn't know he was in my bed that night. I woke up to find him there, and Kash …" I stopped and took a calming breath.

I'd already told Kash what had happened that night. I didn't have to tell Bane.

"Is that so? That's your story now?" The mocking way he said it sent a wave of anger through me.

He hadn't been there. He had no idea what I'd been through with Pirate.

"I never did anything with Pirate," I said through clenched teeth. "Except live in a constant state of fear that he'd touch me again." I snapped my mouth shut, furious with myself for saying anything more. I'd held this secret in for years, and now it seemed to be coming out like vomit when I opened my mouth.

"What does that mean?"

I wasn't telling him any more. I was done talking about it.

"Decided not to make up a lie after all?" he asked.

I snapped my head back around to glare at him. "I wasn't lying! Yes, I kept Pirate's sick, twisted thing he had for me from Kash because I feared he'd kill him, but I didn't do it to save Pirate. I hated my brother. I did it to protect Kash." I paused and took a deep breath, then blew it out. "But I couldn't. And in the end, I protected him the only way I knew how. I loved Kash. I would never have betrayed him."

I turned to look out the passing trees, not wanting to see Bane's reaction to my truth. I didn't care if he didn't believe me. Kash had.

"If you loved him, if you still care, then stay away from him. Make no contact. You aren't what he needs."

If that was true, then it was a cruel twist of fate that Kash Savelle was the only person I would always need.

The one-bedroom apartment had a kitchen and living room in an open layout with one bathroom in the hallway and a bedroom at the other end. It was located in a safe area, clean, with extra security, requiring a key card to get in the main door of the building and the elevator. I wouldn't have been able to afford something like this even if I'd stayed and worked for Glenda an entire year.

Bane had dropped me here just over two hours since he had picked me up at Glenda's. If anything, the man was efficient. After he opened the door to the apartment, handed me the key card, he told me to have a nice life and that he never wanted to see me again. I nodded, and he turned and left. Like he had said, a key fob to a Ford of some kind was on the counter, and there were three separate sets of papers stapled together and an envelope. The first set of papers had information about my job, which was working as a front-desk administrator at a doctor's office and a salary that made my jaw drop. I had to read it three times, then sat down.

Eighty-five thousand dollars a year was insane. What would I do with that much? My head was still reeling from that when I looked at the next set of papers, which detailed my lease and contact info for the company that owned the building if I had any issues. Last, it was a bank account welcome packet. My account number and current balance of ten thousand dollars.

"What the hell?" I gasped.

Reaching for the envelope, I opened it to find a debit card for my bank account and a book of checks. There was also a small key that looked like it belonged to a mail slot.

Shaking my head in disbelief, I sat there, letting this all sink in. I no longer had to hide or run. Arthur was never going to find me here, nor was my father. I wouldn't be sleeping in a box on the street. I should be relieved. Thrilled. Yet misery sat heavy on my chest. This was a payoff. An oddly generous one. They could have dumped me on the side of the road and driven away. Yet they had made sure I was safe and secure. Why? For Kash? Had he asked Bane to do this? Maybe this was his goodbye.

The truth had come years too late. His heart wasn't mine anymore. When he'd held me, it was for the loss of the girl he had once loved. Unlike the night in the woods, that had been his closure.

Dropping the papers onto the cushion beside me, I closed my eyes and allowed the tears to once again fall.

NINETEEN
KASH

The office was tidy. Annoyingly so. There wasn't anything out of place. It smelled faintly of cologne, which was the only sign that someone had ever spent time in here. Otherwise, it appeared ready for a photo op at any moment. I picked up a pen from the container on his desk that held five of the same kind. Nothing terribly expensive, but uniform. Flipping it through my fingers, I looked over at Gathe, who was going through the bookshelf that was packed with self-help and business books. He smirked at one of them and tossed it over onto the desk.

The title said *Can't Hurt Me*.

"Ironic," Gathe said with a chuckle.

Than stood over in the other corner of the room, texting.

We'd arrived in Little Rock a little after midnight. I'd decided on the four-hour drive that we were going to play a little psychological game with him first. Besides, it gave me more time to find out all I needed to know.

There was no one else in the building, but we had entered it around six this morning. Arthur Howt rented this private office space and had no employees of his own. He built websites for new businesses that couldn't afford the larger firms. The balance of his bank accounts told me that he wasn't very good at it. He was behind on his rent here, his apartment rent, and his car payment. Yet, last week, he'd gone on a cigar tasting trip with friends to Cuba. Money management was not his thing.

The sound of footsteps approached, and Than looked up from his phone, his eyes going from the door to me. I, too, turned my attention to the door.

Gathe held out another book and glanced at me. "Sounds like we got company," he whispered, then grinned.

The key slid into the lock with a click; then the handle turned, and the door swung open. Arthur Howt came striding in while talking with the phone pressed to his ear.

"She exists. I paid you up front, more money than you are worth. Either find her or I'm going to—"

His words came to a halt just as his gaze landed on me sitting in the chair behind his desk. He swung his gaze to Than and then Gathe.

"I'm sorry, but who are you, and why are you in my office? If there is some kind of maintenance being done, I wasn't informed, and I did not approve of you being in here," he said sternly.

Than ducked his head, chuckling, as he ran his thumb under hit bottom lip.

"Please, finish your phone call," I said.

His gaze was back to me. He ended it and started to slip it into his pocket.

"Ah, we'll be taking that," I told him, motioning at Gathe to get the phone.

His bravado showed its first crack as Gathe sauntered over to him and snatched his phone easily enough.

"You can't take my phone!" he shouted, glancing back at the door, as if hoping someone might hear him.

"The building is closed today," I informed him. "All others were notified that there was a rodent infestation found in the basement and it must be fumigated."

He shook his head. "I didn't get that call."

"We know," Than replied.

Arthur narrowed his gaze, trying again to appear unafraid. But his eyes told another story.

"You've got shit taste in books," Gathe said, tossing one onto the floor and picking up another one to pretend to look over.

"I'm going to call the police," he threatened, stalking over to the desk and watching me closely as he jerked the landline up. When he realized I wasn't going to stop him, he turned to the other two while pressing 911. "You all need to leave."

The confusion in his expression would have been comical if I wasn't barely containing myself from ripping him apart with my bare hands. He pressed the phone to his ear finally and started to open his mouth to speak when he was met with the silence.

"That infestation took out the phone lines in the building," I told him.

His arm slowly lowered as he put the phone back down.

"Why are you here?" he asked, his eyes darting to each of us.

"I'll be the one asking the questions," I told him and let his pen fall from my knuckles to his desk. "Who are you looking for?" I asked him.

He appeared to not understand me.

"The phone call," I reminded him. "You paid to find someone."

He let out a nervous short laugh. "Oh, that is just family issues."

I stood then. "What kind of family issues?"

He took a step toward the door. He was planning on running. The survival instinct that all humans had.

Gathe was faster though and dropped another book before stepping between the exit and Arthur.

Panic flashed across his face. "Look, if this is about money, I'm broke. I have nothing."

"If it were only that simple," Than said.

"What do you want then?" His voice trembled this time as he spoke.

"So many things," Gathe said with a sigh. "I could go for a chicken biscuit, for starters."

That almost made me smile.

"What?" Arthur asked, looking at Gathe, as if trying to decide if he was all there or not.

"You've never heard of a chicken biscuit? Are there no Chick-fil-A's in Arkansas?"

Arthur looked from Gathe to me. "Is it drugs? Are you all looking for something so you can buy more?"

"I thought I told you I was going to ask the questions," I replied as I walked around the desk and in his direction.

He moved toward the wall slightly but stopped.

"Who in your family are you looking for?"

He licked his lips nervously. "My, uh, niece."

I took another step toward him.

"I'd say that's a very loose description," Than said, swinging his gaze from the window back to Arthur, who was now locked on him.

"What do you know about it?" he asked Than.

Than raised his brows slightly and cut his eyes to me.

"We know that you don't have a niece. Your sister has no children of her own."

Arthur paused. "She has a stepdaughter. Problem child. What business is that of yours, and how do you know this about my sister?"

I laughed then, hearing the sinister lilt to it as I did. "Child? Oh, Cressida hasn't been a child in a long time. And she was never a problem."

Arthur's eyes widened then, and his bravado was raising its head again at the sound of her name. "You know Cressida?"

"I'd be careful with your tone," I warned him.

"Listen, if she's done something, I can fix it. Just tell me where she is. My sister and brother-in-law are worried sick."

The blatant lies and dark flicker in his eyes pushed me too far. He was slammed against the wall with my hand around his throat before he could finish the sentence.

Now that he was unable to speak now from the lack of oxygen, I bared my teeth as I got in his face. "Lie, and you'll pay for it. I came for the truth."

He shook his head, his eyes no longer hiding his terror as he stared at me. I eased up on my grip just enough so he could speak.

"Why are you looking for her?"

I felt his throat bob under my palm as he swallowed. "Worried," he choked out, and I gripped his neck tighter and slammed the back of his head against the wall again.

"I said, NO LIES!" I snarled.

His eyes were watering, and he was getting the blue hue from not being able to breathe. I gave him enough to keep him from passing out, but dug my fingers into the sides of his neck, needing to cause him pain.

"Try again," I urged.

"Sh-sh-she was mine."

Those words were a mistake on his part. His head hit the wall so hard this time that I heard a crash from the other side of it. He went limp, his head falling to the side.

"You're gonna give him an easy death if you keep that up," Than pointed out.

"It'll be an easier cleanup," Gathe said. "I mean, unless you do it hard enough that his brains start coming out his fucking ears."

I let go of his neck, and he dropped to the ground like a sack of potatoes slumping over to the side.

I then held my hand out to Gathe. "Give me his phone."

Gathe handed it to me, and I broke through the password, then went to his text messages, scrolling for any mention of her.

Cressida's name wasn't mentioned, but it was one of the text threads. Although it had been six months since he'd last texted her. I began reading from the most recent. He was demanding that that she tell him where she went, threatening to have her tossed out on her ass, that he'd turn her father against her. Then, in the next text, he'd apologize, saying he didn't mean it and that he loved her. She never responded to any of it.

Finally, something from her.

> **Arthur: If you don't come tonight and treat me with respect at dinner with our family, I'll make you live to regret it. Your attitude has been unacceptable. All we have done for you, all I have done for you. You get to live in that house because of me. Lucy would have kicked you out years ago.**

Cressida: You can't hurt me.

Arthur: You know I can. And I will do it again just to remind you since you seem to have forgotten.

Cressida: Bruises and broken bones heal.

Arthur: Then perhaps I'll do something more permanent. If you can't obey me and be a good girl, then you're of no use to me. A problem. Clearing you out of our lives might be exactly what we need.

I spun back around to the unconscious man on the floor and went to grab him again. Wanting to see him suffer, scream out in agony.

"You'll regret it if you snap his neck. Clearly, whatever you're reading means he deserves a more brutal exit," Than said through the fog of rage that had taken over me.

I let go of his neck, but not before I threw him onto the floor.

He groaned.

"Oh good, he's not dead yet." Gathe sounded truly relieved.

I glared down at the phone. "We might need to string him up before I read more. Go ahead and move on with the torture part before I kill him right here."

"Slap him until he is alert enough to stand," Than told Gathe. "I'll go get the Escalade and bring it up to the back door."

I stayed back, keeping my distance. If I got too close, I wasn't sure what I'd do to him. And he wasn't worthy of a quick death.

"There he is," Gathe said after the third slap. "We have open eyes, but the condition of his brain function is still iffy."

I watched as Gathe stood back up, dragging Arthur up, too, by one arm. When Arthur saw me, his eyes went wide, and he began to struggle against Gathe's hold.

"Go ahead and pull your arm out of the socket," Gathe told him. "If you haven't figured it out, we don't give a fuck."

"Don-don-don't," he stammered out, then began to whimper.

"Ah shit," Gathe said. "He pissed his pants. I don't want piss on the seats. They'll stink the entire ride home."

"I'll grab a bag out of one of the trash cans out front. He can sit on that," I told him. "Let's go."

I went on ahead of them while Gathe taunted Arthur's struggle to walk and scolded him like a child when he stumbled. The man wailed just before we reached the door, and I glanced back to see Gathe dragging him by the hair of his head. His legs sliding across the floor.

"He's a bad seed," Gathe said, exasperated. "Doesn't fucking know how to listen."

The kitchen was stocked with basic necessities. There were coffee pods for the Keurig, half-and-half, as well as a holiday flavor creamer in the refrigerator, along with eggs, butter, cream cheese, and bagels. I found some other items in the pantry. Taking out the sugar and a loaf of bread, I went about making myself breakfast, although I had no appetite. I realized I'd not eaten at all yesterday either, and I didn't want to meet with my new employer on an empty stomach. I was already going to be tired; at least, I could make sure I wasn't hungry.

Sleep had come for me last night, but it took hours. I had a shower, then sat on the sofa, looking out at the quiet street while the world slept. Somewhere around four, I'd finally gone to bed, which meant I had a solid three hours. I was going to need a lot of concealer today for under my eyes.

While my coffee was brewing, I opened my purse and found a pen, then turned over the papers detailing my new job to write down a list of things I needed to do today other than go to my new place of employment.

The first thing was to get a phone. I glanced over at the envelope that contained my debit card. I didn't want to use any of that money. It wasn't mine. I had done nothing to earn it.

Taking the pen in my hand, I wrote down, *Go get a new bank account.*

I could put the money I did have in it and leave the other alone. I would find a way to send the ten thousand back to Bane Cash. But that was something I would figure out later. I had more pressing matters.

Walking over to get my cup of coffee, I went about fixing it up with cream and sugar, took the bagel I had toasted with cream cheese, and went to sit at the small two-person table. I was back to being alone. Looking around at the bare walls and lack of holiday decorations, I sighed heavily. This was my life. I wasn't on the streets. Arthur wasn't a threat. No one was going to control me here. I wouldn't get a broken wrist if I didn't behave the way I had been instructed.

Yet my heart was still heavy with something beyond pain. There was a deep sorrow that took the ability to feel any joy about anything. I had learned to survive without Kash, and I knew I could do it again.

Bane wanted me to stay away from Mississippi and Kash. He didn't have to worry about that. I never wanted to see either again. Both always left me broken.

This wasn't what I had expected. When I'd read what my salary was going to be, I'd imagined a large doctor's office with several doctors. But here I stood, behind the front desk, with my only coworker being a six-month-old golden Lab named Rocket. He bumped my leg, and I smiled down at him. I'd given him two of the doggy treats that we had out for patients who brought their dogs in with them. The little cutie was working his charm for more.

I bent don't to scratch behind his ear as he wagged his tail furiously. "I was told you only get two in the morning and one in the afternoon," I told him. "I don't need to make Dr. Carmichael mad at me on my very first day."

That was another thing that had surprised me. It was the doctor, Neil Carmichael, who met me at the door this morning and showed me around. He also gave me a list of things to do that were simple instructions on answering the phone, booking appointments, and finding files. His first patient had walked in, carrying a homemade apple pie in one hand and a small toy-sized fluff ball of a dog in her other.

Since then, I had booked several appointments, changed a few, emailed the elementary school a student's vaccine records, pulled six different patient files, and been given a box of fruitcake cookies by a patient who had stopped in just to deliver goodies.

How had Bane found me a job like this? I doubted he knew Dr. Carmichael personally. I mean, why would he? A doctor with his own practice in another state.

Rocket nudged my leg again when I straightened back up to take the last patient's file and put it back in the cabinet. He was going to be good for me. I'd managed to smile and even laugh once at his antics. There was something to this therapy-dog thing.

The phone rang, and I went to answer it.

"Dr. Carmichael's office," I said. "How may I help you?"

"Yes, I need to speak to a Cressida Beck," a woman replied.

"That's me," I answered hesitantly because no one knew I had this job except Bane and the rest of the Southern Mafia, I assumed.

"Oh, okay. Well, your phone is ready to be picked up. We are open until five today."

My phone? I hadn't gone to get a phone yet. Opening the bank account had taken all my time this morning.

"I, uh, don't know what you're talking about."

"The iPhone 17 … you wanted the lavender one, and all we had in stock was black. I had to have one sent to us from another store …" She trailed off, then added, "You already paid for it." As if that would jog my memory.

I knew I hadn't paid for anything. Bane or Kash must have. The fact that it was lavender, my favorite color? Only Kash would know that. The pang I'd tried to push away while focusing on work and Rocket was back. This was his doing. All of it. I didn't want that damn phone either.

"I, uh … I don't want it," I blurted a little too harshly I realized.

Silence. She clearly didn't know what to do about that.

"Can you just refund whatever card it was charged to?" I asked her.

"No, I can't. It was paid in cash. You gave me the cash … I mean, I thought it was you who had come in and opened the new account."

A female had done this? Who had Kash sent to do it?

"It wasn't me. It was a friend," I told her.

"Oh, well, I'm not sure what you want me to do. But the phone is in your name, and the contract is signed … by you. Or who I thought was you." She was as confused as I was.

Dammit, Kash. You could have just told me goodbye. Spoken to me. Allowed me some form of closure. This is more painful than if you'd done it to my face.

"Fine. I can't pick it up today though. I work until five."

"We can have it dropped off at your office if you would like," she said. "Dr. Carmichael's, correct? On Broad Street?"

My eyes narrowed as I stared straight ahead. "How do you know that?"

"Uh, it's on your account," she replied.

Of course it was. I was gripping the phone so tight that it was starting to sting my hand. "Yes. Then if it can be brought to me, that will be fine."

"Great! I'll have someone bring it then." She was clearly relieved.

"Thank you," I told her, then ended the call.

It had been easier when I thought Bane had done all this. The Mafia wanting to get rid of me was one thing. Kash wanting to was another.

It was a cut I hadn't wanted to accept, but I had to now.

TWENTY-ONE
KASH

I stood in front of Arthur Howt as his head slowly bobbed with his struggle to hold it up. Blood dripped from his ears, nose, and mouth. He was starting to choke on it too. Once he had begged me not to kill him and admitted to the things I'd read him in the texts he had with Cressida, I'd gone a touch mad. Whatever control I'd been trying to hold on to vanished, and I'd seen red.

I wasn't sure he was even aware of his surroundings anymore. His eyes were a touch vacant. But he did still whimper when I took my knife to him. He was feeling pain if nothing else.

"We gonna leave him strung up here? Or ditch the body elsewhere?" Than asked.

The abandoned mine we'd brought him to was one that I'd been in before. Two years ago, several of the guys in the Alabama branch had been sent to help the Arkansas branch handle an issue. The issue had been brought here and tortured until he talked. No one came here. It was closed due to safety issues and illegal to mine in. While the Arkansas branch took their victim's body parts to feed the hogs, I didn't want to spend the time doing so, nor did I trust them not to report our being here to Linc.

"Yeah. He can hang here and rot. The Arkansas branch will find him eventually and dispose of what's left," I replied.

"Sweet. So, we're about done? Not sure he's mentally with us anymore," Gathe said as he lit a cigarette that he had clenched between his teeth.

"Yeah. We're about done."

I stepped up closer to the bastard who had hurt Cressida both physically and emotionally. He made a gasping sound, then a gurgle as blood came from his mouth.

"You touched what belonged to me. My little Songbird was broken at your hands. She survived you. Escaped you. And I'll take care of her now. You can go to hell, knowing she won. She defeated you. And that sweet body she would never give you? I've had it. I had it first, and I'll have it last. She gives it to me. She wants my cock. Those pretty legs spread for me."

I smirked as hatred glinted in his eyes. He was still in there. He understood. I grabbed his face, squeezing his cheeks together as more blood ran from his nose and the corner of his mouth.

"I'll see you in hell, you son of a bitch," I drawled, then took the blade in my hand and slid it right between his ribs. The exact way I'd taken Pirate's life four years ago.

The struggle to breathe was instant for him, and I twisted the knife in his lung that I'd punctured, watching his wide-eyed panic when he realized he was going to choke to death.

"And there he goes," Gathe drawled as the fight in his eyes slowly faded until as did the sounds of him struggling to breathe.

"Are you gonna tell her he was the one who killed her mother?"

I wasn't sure. That was information I didn't think he'd meant to divulge. The affair that Cressida's father had been having and his refusal to leave his wife because of her emotional state had led to the current Mrs. Beck bribing her brother with Cressida one day being his if he killed her mother and made it look like an accident. I wasn't sure Cressida needed to know that. I'd gotten her revenge for her.

"Are we gonna kill the stepmom too? Because if we are, I suggest putting some time between the two deaths," Than said.

I turned and walked back toward them. "No. But I'm going to make sure her sins are revealed and she pays for her crime. She has to suffer, too, but I'll let the law handle that one."

"Thank fuck. I hate killing women. Even terrible bitches like that one," Gathe said, falling into step beside me.

We walked out of the mine into the evening air. I was ready to get back to Madison, clean the bastard's blood off me, and go see my little Songbird. Reassure myself she was safe.

The sight of Bane's truck outside my house when I finally pulled in the next morning wasn't what I wanted to deal with right now. I'd texted Cressida ten times, and she'd not responded once. I'd called, and it would only beep once, then start recording for a message. No ringing. Nothing.

Bane being here meant he was aware I'd left town and possibly why. Dammit. Leaving Cressida and going back to Alabama was not happening. Not yet. I needed more time to figure out how to stay. How to have her too. Yes, I'd acted out of rage four years ago, and if Cressida hadn't lied, I would have very likely gone to prison. But I hadn't. She'd protected me, and I hadn't protected her. I sure as fuck wasn't leaving her unprotected anymore.

Why couldn't I have her? What was it the family's business? So I'd killed a man over her. I could tick off at least ten family members who had killed a man because of a woman. Yeah, maybe I'd been too young to feel what I did for Cressida, but four years later, and I still felt it. All of it. Just as strong as I had back then.

Opening the front door, I stalked inside, ready to face whatever bullshit was waiting on me. I had barely gotten inside the foyer when Bane stepped through the open entrance of the parlor on the left to face me. His arms were crossed over his chest, and the scowl on his face just pissed me off. I wasn't dealing with him. He wasn't the boss. If Linc had a problem with me, then send him.

I met his scowl with one of my own but kept walking passed him.

"Kash!" Oz's sharp tone stopped me.

I didn't want to fight with my brother, but if he was siding with his best friend over me, I would.

"What?" I asked, spinning back around to glare at them both.

"Why were you in Arkansas?" Bane demanded.

He knew where I had been, but not why. The son of a bitch had a tracker on me. I'd left the phone they knew I had here and taken a burner with me. That meant he had one planted elsewhere. We'd left my truck at Gathe's and rented an Escalade so the tracker had to be on me somewhere.

"Did you put it in my fucking boot?" I asked.

He didn't respond. "Why were you in Arkansas?"

I was tired. I wanted to see Cressida. And my temper was short because of both. I took a deep breath and tried to calm down. Yelling at Bane wasn't going to help matters.

"I had some business to handle."

"What business?" he snapped.

"Personal. Last I checked, we are allowed a personal life. I don't have to report to anyone about that."

"You do when you go to the city your former girlfriend lived for the past four years," Bane replied.

"Why is that?" I asked, taking a step back toward him. "Huh? Yeah, Cressida lived there. She's not there now. So, what did I do that makes this your business? Linc doesn't seem to care. He's not here."

"Linc is letting me handle this," he replied.

"Why? Because it involves your best friend's younger brother? Or because he thinks it's a waste of time? There is no reason for all this ... this fucking ... monitoring. Pirate is dead. I can't kill him again. What is it you're worried I'll do?"

Bane's phone buzzed, and he pulled it out of his pocket and answered it. "Yeah?" He didn't take his eyes off me, as if I were going to run. This was all too over-the-top dramatic. "Fuck," he muttered, and anger thinned his lips. "Yeah, go ahead and clean it up. Thanks," he said, then ended the call and shoved his phone into his pocket. "This. This is why I was monitoring you. This was why you couldn't be near her. You act without consequence or reason."

"What did he do?" Oz asked, stepping up beside him. Concern marring his brow.

"Howi and Avett found a dead man sliced up and hanging up in the abandoned mine they use for their underground. Identified him as Arthur Howt," Bane said, turning his hard glare at me. "Cressida Beck's step uncle."

Oz ran a hand through his hair and sighed.

"He broke her bones, beat her, punished her to control and manipulate her. She was here because she had run from the narcissistic bastard," I informed them. "He also killed her mother. Something she doesn't know. She found her mother drowned in a hot tub. Thinks she passed out from mixing antidepressants and alcohol. Yeah, I killed the son of a bitch."

Some of the anger in Bane's expression eased, and he glanced at my brother, who was staring at me. He wasn't angry, but something was wrong. It was … he seemed … pained or sad. It was odd, considering the situation.

"All right. He deserved to die," Bane replied. "But taking Than and Gathe and sneaking off to do it, then leaving his corpse for the Arkansas branch to clean up wasn't the correct way to handle it. That's the problem with your obsession with Cressida. You don't think clearly. That is shit that will get you killed. Or someone else killed."

"I want to talk to Linc. Have him talk to Hughes. I want to come home. The threat of my killing Pirate is over. The case was close and sealed."

"We all want that. And Blaise has agreed to it," Oz said, still with a tone that didn't make sense, much like his expression.

"I get to stay?" I asked, hope surging through my chest.

Bane nodded. "Yeah, you do. But …" He paused for a moment. "Cressida is gone. Contact with her is off-limits. She is your crazy trigger, and before you can start getting as deep in with her as you once were, she's been moved out of your reach."

The words sank in slowly, but my move to get in Bane's face was much faster. His shoulders might be wider than mine, but I was an inch taller and not scared of the motherfucker.

"WHERE IS SHE?!" I roared as my temples began to pound.

"Jesus Christ, KASH!" Oz shouted, grabbing my collar and jerking me back.

Bane's entire body had gone rigid, but there wasn't fury glinting in his eyes, like I'd expected, but sympathy.

What the fuck?! He didn't get to feel fucking sorry for me!

"Where. IS. SHE?" I demanded, pulling free of Oz's hold.

"She is safe. Provided for. I made sure she had all she needed. Including a good job." Bane's tone was reassuring, as if that was all I needed to hear.

"Tell me where!" I started at him again, and Oz's hand clamped down on my shoulder, stopping me.

How the fuck was he so goddamn strong?

"Let go of me," I sneered.

"This is why you can't be around her, Kash. Listen to yourself. She makes you psycho," Oz said.

"No. Her being taken away and hidden from me is making me psycho. This goddamn family I didn't ask to be born into is making me psycho! Now tell me where she is!"

Bane blew out a heavy breath, and his gaze looked past me toward my brother, who was still holding on to me.

"Someone needs to start talking," I warned them. "What if someone took Halo from you?" I asked Bane. "Or Winslet from you?" I asked my brother. "You'd both lose your goddamn mind."

"Not the same," Bane told me. "Halo is my world. My center. My calm. She is also my wife."

"Who you get to keep protected. Safe. You don't have to worry about anyone hurting her. That's not a threat you face, but you can't tell me if someone hurt her, you wouldn't show your own version of crazy. She wasn't always your wife, but before she took your last name, did you love her less?"

He shook his head. "No, but I don't just love Halo. She saved me. Brought me back from the darkness that I didn't think I'd ever return from after losing Crosby. She owns me. Without her, I have no soul."

"I wanted to come home," I snarled. "I thought being home meant Madison. My family. But I saw her again. Nothing had changed for me." Stabbing my chest with my pointer finger, I leaned closer to Bane. "My home isn't a fucking town, and it's not family. Because the moment I looked into her eyes again was when I felt it. Home. SHE is my home."

Bane was looking at my brother again, who had remained silent through it all. Not trying to convince me he loved Winslet more than I loved Cressida.

"I'm sorry," Oz said behind me. "But right now, we need you focused. She doesn't focus you. She distracts you."

"Her being taken from me fucking distracts me!" I yelled and jerked free of his hold to turn and look at him.

What was his deal? Why did he look so goddamn torn up? Was this because he didn't agree with them taking Cressida, but wasn't going to admit it?

"Mom has stage four liver cancer." Oz's voice cracked as he said it.

The oxygen felt as if it had been sucked from the room.

"What?" I asked.

I hadn't heard him right. I couldn't have.

"She thought she was allergic to something she was eating. She was having abdominal pain." His words came out hoarse. "It got better when she cut out her glass of wine in the evening, but that was short-lived. Then there was swelling, and she went in for testing."

I shook my head. "No," I said. "No."

The emotion on his face, the pain in his expression, his silence—it all made sense now.

"What?" I asked. "What does the doctor say? I mean, what about treatments? How are they going to get rid of it?"

Oz glanced at Bane, and I didn't like that. When his gaze came back to me, I saw the answers I did not want to hear. The sorrow was deep.

"Stage four means it's spread beyond the liver. It isn't curable, but there are treatments to slow its progression. Prolong her life."

I took several steps back until I had the wall behind me for support. "But we can afford the best treatments."

"Yes. And she will be getting them. But all the money and connections in the world can't cure cancer." Oz's words came out raspy. "She wants you home. Her baby boy under her roof. She wants her Christmas to be happy. She needs you to be here. With us. Not going psycho over your obsession with a girl. Please, Kash, give her that. Let Cressida go. For now at least."

In all my life, I knew I'd never face anything as unfair again. Being asked to choose between the woman who had given me life, loved me, raised me, who was the only gentleness I had known, growing up, who needed me while her body turned on her, and the one girl who had stolen my soul seven years ago and would own it until the day I died.

TWENTY-TWO
KASH

The past week, we had started having family breakfasts together. Forge, Oz, and Winslet all came, and we sat around the dining room table, the way we had growing up. Mom didn't look sick, but Dad had said that once she started treatments, things would change. She was going to undergo some cutting-edge treatments that had been personalized for her specific condition. The doctors had wanted to start her on them immediately, but she'd said she wanted to wait until after Christmas.

We all had one goal now, and it was to make this holiday perfect for her. I felt guilty for the fact that I hadn't even noticed my parents' absence so much since I'd gotten home. I'd been so preoccupied with being back, then finding ways to see Cressida that I didn't question my parents not being around. They had been seeing a specialist and going over the process that would start the day after Christmas. Oz had said it had taken Dad to get her to agree not to wait until the new year, like she'd wanted to.

My dad had gotten on his knees and wept. I'd never seen him cry. None of us had. Oz said he had to walk out of the room before he fell apart, watching it. The sight had changed Mom's mind. She'd agreed for Dad's sake.

Now we were all pretending like life was grand while watching my mother barely touch her food, my dad rarely taking his eyes off her. It was as if he was afraid if he did, something would happen to her.

We were two days away from Christmas now, and I was going through the motions of life. The hole in my chest had morphed into a dark, endless well of misery. I didn't want to hear another fucking Christmas song or be around any kind of joy-filled people. But for Mom, I watched the holiday movies she loved at night. No longer leaving the house much, except go see lights with her or run and get her something that she might want to eat.

Dad wasn't leaving her side.

Forge had moved into his old bedroom, and starting tonight until Christmas, Oz and Winslet were staying in his childhood room that was now a guest bedroom with a king-size bed. The scenario of us all sleeping under the same roof again was one I would never have imagined, but then I'd never thought I'd face losing my mother. Not at this age at least. She was supposed to be old and enjoying spoiling her grandkids, watching them grow, being there for all the important things.

I sat on the edge of my bed after leaving the breakfast table and hung my head. My mom was sick, and the only person I wanted right now I couldn't have. I couldn't even talk to. I had no fucking idea where Bane had taken her. Was she happy with her new life? Job? Had she made friends? Or was she alone this Christmas?

"Fuck!" I growled, fisting my hair in my hands.

A knock on the door caused my head to snap up, and I expected Mom, not wanting her to see me wallowing in my constant state of misery, when Oz opened the door, then stepped inside.

I didn't want to see him. I had to blame someone. I needed to place my rage somewhere, and he and Bane were the two I'd sunk it into.

"Get out," I snarled.

I acted for Mom's sake, but she wasn't in here right now.

Oz didn't leave but walked over to me. I straightened, glaring up at him as he got closer. He needed to get the hell out of my room.

"I said, get the—"

He held out a piece of torn paper. "Here," he interrupted me. "Merry Christmas."

My eyes dropped to the paper, and I stared at it, then snatched it from his grasp. There was a phone number scribbled out on it.

"Whose number is this?" I asked, studying it, memorizing it in case he took it back.

"I said, merry Christmas, didn't I? Whose do you think it is?"

I closed it up tightly in my hand, pulling it closer to my chest, and studied him before asking, "Cressida?"

If it wasn't, I might put the lamp beside me through a wall for the small sliver of hope he'd given me, then taken away.

He nodded. "Yeah. But that's all. Just contact. Don't go find her. Stay here. Christmas is in a couple of days. Let Mom have this. Then we'll go see Linc."

"Linc? I thought this was all Bane's doing?"

"Bane was doing this for us. Our family. He's the only one who knew about it. We were keeping it quiet until you and Forge were told. Bane only did what I'd asked him to do."

"Thanks," I said sarcastically. "Good to know who I need to blame."

Oz didn't respond, but gave me a tight smile, then turned and walked out of the room. The door hadn't clicked shut before I grabbed my phone and dialed the number he'd given me. My pulse raced as it began to ring.

TWENTY-THREE
CRESSIDA

The same number flashed on my screen. That was the third time in a row. I knew the area code, and I did not want to speak to anyone from Madison, Mississippi. I turned off my ringer on the first ring and went back to the mail that had been delivered. Sorting out the junk from the bills. Dr. Carmichael had told me that unless a catalog interested me to toss it along with all other "offers," then leave the rest of the mail on his desk.

My eyes kept going back to my phone, like a glutton for punishment. This time, when it lit up, it was a text message. Nope. Not reading that either. If it was Bane checking in, he could ask Dr. Carmichael how I was doing. And if it was Kash … well … I was protecting myself. He only brought me heartache. I was sad enough as it was. I didn't need for it to get worse.

"This one is a doggy treats catalog," I told Rocket, holding it up. "We might have to give it a look and see if there is any-thing you might need."

He cocked his head to the side, like he often did with his tongue hanging out, as if he was hanging on my every word. I went over to leave the doggy catalog on my desk, and he followed behind me. It was rare he wasn't at my heels. Dr. Carmichael had said yesterday that he believed his dog would rather go home with me. I wouldn't object, but he'd been joking. He wasn't about to give me his dog.

Perhaps I should get one of my own. I could use the company. It was lonely in the evenings and weekends. I'd bought some decorations for the apartment with my first paycheck this past weekend, and that had given me something to do at least.

The door opened to the office, and I looked up to see Rhodes—I forgot his last name—the guy who owned the gym three doors down, walk inside. He'd brought in someone last Thursday who had hurt their wrist on one of the machines in his gym. While Dr. Carmichael was checking the injured man over, Rhodes had leaned against the counter and talked to me.

To be exact, he flirted with me.

Before he had left, he asked me if I was free on Friday or Saturday night, and I told him I had plans, which included decorating and then watching *Stranger Things* on Netflix. Friday, he returned with a stack of one-week-free coupons to put out on our counter and asked what time I took a lunch. I'd told him that I had to file during my lunch hour that day. And now, he was back two hours after opening on Monday morning.

Great. I needed to think up another excuse fast.

"Good morning," I said.

"Morning, beautiful," he replied with a crooked grin.

It most likely worked for him a lot. That grin thing. He owned a gym. Worked out all day. He looked like a bodybuilder. His face wasn't bad either, but I did not want anything to do with a man again. I was still broken from the only one I'd wanted.

I didn't know how to respond to the beautiful comment, so I continued my fake smile. "How can we help you today?" *Since you're clearly not injured and you don't have an injured client with you.*

He put an elbow on the counter and leaned slightly closer to me. "I've got tickets to *A Christmas Carol* musical currently playing at the theater. They put it on every year. You'd like it," he said. "And I'd take you to dinner before, of course."

He was relentless.

I was broken.

Wrong tree, pal.

"Uh, well …" I sighed. "I'm going to be honest with you. I just got out of a …" I paused. That was a lie. *But how did one explain what Kash and I were? I just got shipped off here by the guy I love who no longer loves me?* That just sounded pathetic.

"Relationship," he supplied.

I hesitated, then nodded. Whatever. He didn't need my backstory.

"Me too," he replied. "Three years, and she left me for her ex-husband."

Oh. Ouch.

"I'm sorry about that," I stammered awkwardly.

"Yeah, I'm not. We had run our course. Time to move on." He winked. "What about we just have a night out, getting to know each other?"

I glanced over at my phone to see six text messages now. "Uh, I'm sorry. There seems to be an issue. I've got several text messages from a friend back home." I gave him an apologetic smile. "Maybe after I've had some space and time. I'm just not ready. But thank you."

His disappointment was clear, but at least he wasn't leaning on the counter now. "All right. But when you're ready, I'm right down the street."

I nodded. *I know, and I do not care.*

"Come in, and I'll give you the first month free," he offered.

Not happening.

"That's very generous of you."

He seemed to brighten up at that, and I waved, then turned my back to him and picked up my phone. I was going to ignore this, but my willpower was shot. I wanted to see who had been texting and calling me.

I clicked the text message alerts from the number and scrolled up to the first one.

> Unknown: Cressida, it's Kash. Please answer your phone.

> Unknown: I just want to hear your voice. Please.

> Unknown: Songbird, you're killing me.

> Unknown: I am begging you.

> Unknown: I need to talk to you.

> Unknown: Don't punish me. I didn't know Bane had taken you. No one will tell me where you are. Oz gave me this number, and it's all I have. Please talk to me.

He didn't know? But … the lavender phone. Bane wouldn't have cared about my favorite color, much less known what it was.

I chewed up my bottom lip, rereading the text several times before I decided to respond.

> Me: I'm at work.

137

I hit Send, and dots immediately appeared. Had he been sitting there, staring at his phone?

Kash: I need to talk to you.

Shit! Why did he have so much power over me? My heart was already racing in my chest, and the first smallest hint of anything close to happiness was starting up.

Me: I can't talk while I am at work.

I let my finger hover over the Send key and debated saying more, like *I will call you this evening*. But I didn't need to say that. I shouldn't call him. Hearing his voice would only hurt more.

Kash: What time do you get off?

Dammit.

Me: Five.

Kash: I'll call you then. Are you okay? Safe?

I was safe, but I hadn't been okay in years. What did that mean? Okay. If it meant breathing, then sure. I was okay.

Me: I'm safe. I have a good job. I like it. I've made a friend.

I hit Send and left out the fact that my friend was a canine.

Kash: At five, answer your phone.

Bossy. I set the phone down, not bothering to respond to his command. But I'd answer. Just like I hadn't made it thirty

138

minutes before reading his text. I had no control over my actions when it came to Kash.

Dr. Carmichael had received a call on his cell phone just after three and had to leave immediately for a personal house visit. He had a few clients, I'd learned, that he went to them. They didn't come here. He never took any files with him when he went either. I didn't ask since it wasn't my business, but I admit the way he responded so promptly was intriguing.

I'd had to call and reschedule the last two appointments he had coming in after three. With the office closed, I had been able to do all the evening straightening-up without interruption. When five o'clock hit, I was already back at my apartment, standing in the living room, staring at my phone.

It rang immediately.

I took a deep breath, blew it out, then hit Accept.

"Hello?" I said without any trace of emotion, which I felt rather proud of since I was experiencing a swarm of them at the moment.

"Songbird." Kash's sigh of relief as he said my name sure sounded as if he hadn't known where I was. I wanted to believe that. "Where are you?"

"I'm struggling to believe that you didn't know about my relocation," I told him.

"I swear to God I didn't know. I left town for twenty-four hours to handle something, and when I came back, you were gone. Bane wouldn't tell me. No one would!"

I knew if I let myself believe him, I would once again be vulnerable. But he sounded so pained. Desperate.

"Okay," I relented. "Sure."

"Tell me where you are," he urged.

ABBI GLINES

But if I did. He'd come here. And Bane would find out.
They'd either take me off somewhere and dump me or relo-
cate me again. I liked my job. I might not be given a job, a
car, and a place to live the next time. Kash didn't have the
power to protect me. Not from the Mafia family he had been
born into.

"I can't," I finally said.

"Ignore whatever Bane said to you," Kash told me.

But I couldn't. I had no one in this world. It was just me,
and I was never going to move on and make a life for myself
if Kash kept walking into it and shattering the small bits of
security that I'd found.

"It's not about Bane or anything he said. It's about me. I
need to do what is best for me," I said as a lump formed in
my throat.

"And that's not me." It wasn't a question. It was a statement. His words sounded as if I'd just landed a crushing blow
to his chest.

My throat and eyes burned.

"We aren't good for each other." I forced the words out.
Words I didn't want to accept.

"That's not true."

"Your family won't allow it. They don't want you with me,
and your family isn't an ordinary one. You can't defy them.
Neither of us can. You know that. And my heart can't take
having you, only to lose you again." My voice cracked as I
stifled a sob.

"I won't let them." His words were fierce.

"You don't have a choice," I whispered. "If you love or
loved me, then please let me go."

I ended the call before he could say more. He could convince me there was a chance for us again even though I knew
there wasn't. He wanted his life in Madison back, and if he

came here, he'd lose that. Unlike me, he had a home, and I wouldn't let him make the mistake of losing it because of me again.

TWENTY-FOUR
KASH

So many goddamn voices. All the false laughter and pretend cheer. None of it was real. Watching them all, I'd started to become numb. It was the only way I'd managed to get through the past two days. I wasn't a fucking actor, but both my brothers had missed their calling.

Tomorrow, however, was the last day of this. Christmas would come and go, and then my parents would leave for Texas, where Mom would begin her treatments. Forge had decided that he was staying at the house with me. I didn't want him here. I wanted to be left alone.

"Kash." My mother's voice stopped me. I'd been trying to sneak away after the big family dinner.

"Yeah, Mom?" I asked, turning around.

I hadn't noticed the weight loss when I first got home or the little things, like how she appeared almost frail. She was holding on to the banister at the moment, and her knuckles were white from her gripping it so hard. Had walking up the stairs been that hard for her? What else was she covering up for our sake?

"What's wrong?" she asked.

I shook my head. "Nothing. I'm good," I assured her, walking over for my peace of mind in case her legs gave out on her and pulling her into a hug. "I'm good," I repeated again. "Just needed a little alone time."

When I pulled back from hugging her, I didn't let go of her arms. "If you want me down there though, I'll go. We can head down now."

She reached up and patted my cheek, as if I were still a little boy. "My beautiful boy," she said with a soft sad smile. "You never could get away with a lie. Not the way your brothers could. Now, tell me, what has those blue eyes I love so full of sorrow?"

I winced, unable to help it. "Guess I can't pretend it's all okay. And I'm sorry. I'll do better. Let's go down and watch a Christmas movie."

She shook her head. "You're not getting out of this that easy," she said. "I know you're scared, and that's okay. That fear flashes in your gaze every time you look my way. But that's not what I'm talking about. You're … lost. I thought getting to come home and stay would make you happy, but you still have that unsettled glint in them. As if you're searching. What is it for? Hmm? Do you know?"

I squeezed her arms gently. "You don't need to waste energy worrying over me. I'm happy that I get to stay." I couldn't call it home though.

Yes, this had once been my home. She was once my home. But I had grown up, and my home had changed.

"I will worry about you in this life and whatever comes after. It's what mommas do. We want our children happy.

And you've not been truly happy for a long time. But you were once."

Yeah, I'd been happy once. I'd felt like the fucking king of the world.

"I'm happy to be here with you." I told her.

She gave a frown that said she didn't buy my bullshit. "Fine. Keep your secrets. But find what makes you happy and hold on to it. Fight for it."

I nodded. I couldn't tell her it wasn't that easy. My "happy" had blocked my calls and texts. She had refused to talk to me. Asked me to let her go if I loved her. But how was I supposed to do that? I'd walked away four years ago because I thought she'd betrayed me. My hurt and rage had fueled me. With that stripped away, knowing it was me who had betrayed her, me who had shattered both our worlds, I was being eaten alive by the guilt, regret, and anguish.

"There it is again," Mom said softly. "The dark shadows in your gaze. That's what I don't want to see."

If I could make it go away, I would, but she was asking me the one thing I couldn't do for her.

"Come on," I said, linking her arm in mine. "Let's go watch a holiday comedy. I want to hear you laugh. That'll make me happy."

Her hand covered mine, and she patted it. "All right. But I get to pick the movie," she told me.

I sighed dramatically. "Fine. But just this once."

Lying in bed, I stared at the time on my phone, waiting for midnight.

When it came, I texted out, **Merry Christmas, Songbird**. Then hit Send.

I was positive she'd blocked my number, and I could have used another phone, but she'd only block that one too. She wanted me out of her life. My immediate instinct was to do exactly what my mother had said to do—fight. But then I thought about all the pain I'd caused her, and I retreated. She was my home. My happy. But that didn't mean I was hers. I'd destroyed everything else. What if I killed that too?

I started to put my phone down when the ding went off.

Songbird: Merry Christmas, Kash.

Bolting up, I began typing out more and then stopped. I wasn't blocked, but if I pushed too hard, she may stop responding again.

FUCK! I wanted to call her. Hear her voice.

Slowly, I set the phone down and let go of it. That had to be enough for now. It was something. I could hold on to it. Possibly make it through another day of fake joy.

My bedroom door eased open, and my eyes narrowed, unsure who the hell would be coming in my bedroom this late. The moonlight from the windows lit up the area well enough that I could make out my mother's form. I tossed the covers off and stood up. I'd half expected to see Oz here to remind me to make tomorrow good for her. This was concerning. She should be in bed.

"Mom?" I asked, walking over to her.

"Merry Christmas," she said softly.

"Merry Christmas," I replied, still unsure if this was bad or not. "What are you doing up?"

She held out a small gift bag to me, festively wrapped in red and green paper. "You might be grown, but I'm still Santa Claus." Her voice was teasing.

We'd made jokes about that growing up. How Dad always looked as surprised as we were over our gifts on Christmas morning. It had been obvious who Santa was when we all found out the truth behind the myth.

"This couldn't wait until morning? You should be in bed, resting," I told her, taking it.

Her smile was weak, and that scared the shit out of me.

"Not on my busiest night of the year," she told me. Still with the Santa jokes. "Open it." The excited look on her face was almost as if she were the one getting a gift.

I knew whatever she'd brought me wasn't going to bring me any joy, but I'd do my damnedest to smile for her. Pretend the best I could. She might be making visits to all our rooms tonight with presents. Part of her making this Christmas extra special.

The bag was so light that it felt empty. But I opened it and reached inside, only to find what felt like a postcard. I smiled at her because she looked so fucking giddy and hopeful about the odd gift that I wanted to react the way she was hoping.

When I took it out, there was a holiday scene with a little boy and Santa Claus on one side. I flipped it over after glancing up at her to find her eyes twinkling and her hands clasped to her chest. Dropping my gaze back to the card, I read an address. It was in Ocala, Florida.

"There is something else in the bag," she told me.

I reached inside and this time found what felt like a gift card or credit card and pulled it out. It was neither. It was a key card. But to where?

Was I getting transferred to fucking Ocala?! Did they think I wanted that?

"Go get her," Mom urged.

I froze and stared at my mother, processing what she had said. Did she mean …

"Is this …" I was scared to ask. What if I misunderstood?

"Cressida Beck," mom said. "Go get her. She's your happy."

I held up the card. "This is … this is her address?"

She nodded, her eyes glistening and a smile stretching her face. "Yes! The plane is waiting on you at the strip."

What?

"Are you serious?"

She nodded again, almost bouncing on the balls of her feet now.

"How … Dad … Linc …" I stammered.

She grabbed my hands with her much smaller ones. "Your dad has been asking me for months what I wanted for Christmas. I just wanted my family happy and together. But you weren't happy. You were lost. And I told him that until you were happy, I wouldn't be. So, he went to speak to Blaise. Oz went with him. I got my Christmas wish. Now, go get yours."

I stuffed the key and the address into the pockets of my sweatpants, then pulled her into a hug.

"Thank you." My voice sounded tight. The shitstorm of emotions going through me right now had me on the verge of tears.

"Has Santa ever let you down?" she asked.

I smiled then, but the reminder of her reality only made the influx of feelings worse, and I swallowed hard, holding back a fucking sob.

"No, Momma," I said, closing my eyes as I held her. "She sure hasn't."

TWENTY-FIVE
CRESSIDA

I regretted not splurging on a Christmas tree now. Sitting with my cup of nighttime sleepy tea while curled up on the sofa, looking out the window at the other buildings with festive twinkling lights, I wished I had one to wake up to in the morning. It wasn't that this was my first Christmas to be alone. Even living in my father's house, I'd been alone at Christmas. He and Lucy always left on a trip a couple of days before and didn't return until the new year.

But it was my first chance to start new traditions for myself. Make a life that was mine. Where I belonged. Where I didn't feel unwanted. Instead, I was up well past midnight, thinking about Kash and his simple text.

I had blocked his number because I didn't trust myself not to break down and answer him this week. After two glasses of wine, while watching *The Holiday*, I unblocked him. His *Merry Christmas* text came less than an hour later. Which had kept the wine from helping me sleep.

My brain would not shut off, and every memory, good or bad, I had with Kash had decided to replay for me. Remembering the Christmases I'd spent with him. The last holidays I'd had that were happy. He had made them magical. Just being with him. A simple *Merry Christmas* text had broken open the floodgates of the memories I'd tried to repress. Kept locked away. Because they broke me.

The lock sliding open on my door, however, ended my melancholy trip down memory lane. I stared in horror, wondering if I'd imagined it when the handled began to turn. Reaching for my phone to call 911, I jumped up, frantically trying to think of somewhere to hide. But I had nowhere between where I was and the door. I'd have to run toward it to pass it, and there was no time.

The floor lamp that sat to the right of the sofa, I unplugged it and grabbed it to pick up just as the door slowly eased open. Was it someone breaking in, or did they know about me texting Kash? What if this was Bane coming to evict me or … worse?

I had been sitting in the darkness so as to see the Christmas lights outside the window better, so when the form in the darkness moved, I couldn't make out a face until they stepped into the room.

The lamp I had been gripping slid to the floor with a hard thump as Kash's face was illuminated. I stared in disbelief, now wondering if I had, in fact, fallen asleep after all.

He closed the door behind him, not taking his eyes off me. How was he here? He'd said he didn't know where I was. Had that been a lie?

"You're still awake." His voice filled the silence and sent a shiver of pleasure over me.

"Wh-what …" I trailed off, setting the lamp back beside me and stepping around it.

"Santa came early to my house," he replied.

I shook my head, confused. What was he talking about?

He held up a key card, like the one I had for my apartment. "She brought an address and a key to the only thing I wanted."

He wasn't making sense. Who was she?

"I don't … am I dreaming?" I asked, then shook my head. "It's the wine, isn't it?"

The smirk on his face became a chuckle. "No, Songbird, you're not dreaming. But I thought for a moment, I was earlier. Because this was not something I'd imagined getting for Christmas."

I didn't move as Kash walked toward me. He was in my apartment. How? This was bad, wasn't it? If they found out … what would happen to us?

"Kash, you need to leave. If Bane finds out—"

"Fuck Bane. He's on my shit list."

"But he can punish us both for this."

Although, right now, I was thinking it might be worth it. Just to have Kash one more time. Create one last memory. Have one more Christmas that I wanted to remember.

"No, he can't." Kash was still grinning as he reached me. His finger ran down my bare arm, and he looked from where he touched me, then back to meet my gaze. "Like I said, Santa came early, and she trumps them all."

She again.

I shook my head. "Who is she?"

He kept calling Santa she, and that was confusing. Which made me think I was, in fact, asleep.

"My mom." His voice went thick, almost as if he was choking up. "In our house, we always knew that the magic-maker and giver of gifts was my mother. We referred to her as Santa."

Oh. That made sense. There had been a time when my mother was the same.

"Your mom is why you're here?"

He nodded, closing the little space that had been between us. "Yeah," he replied as he cupped the side of my face and began to run the tip of his thumb over my mouth. "She brought me a gift—your address and a key to the apartment—and told me to go get my happy." The corner of his lips quirked then. "So I came to get her."

His happy? I blinked, still not sure how his mother could override the Mafia boss or whoever was making the decisions on keeping us apart.

"She ... she can do that?" I asked, hoping she wasn't going to get in trouble for this.

He nodded. "She can and she did."

Wow. I hadn't realized the women in the family had any power.

"I don't ... I think this might not be real," I whispered.

"I was worried about the same thing on the flight here, but seeing you, it's sinking in. Mom worked her magic." He leaned down and pressed a kiss to the corner of my mouth. "I'd have found you sooner, fought harder, but I couldn't. Not yet. I was having to wait until after Christmas. I'll explain all that later. Right now, I just want to hold you."

Warmth flooded through me as his arms pulled me close, and the heat from his body felt like a balm over my soul.

"Where's your tree?" he asked as he trailed kisses along my jawline.

"I don't have one."

"Mmm ... we need to fix that."

A small laugh bubbled out of me. "It's Christmas Day," I pointed out.

"You're right. I'll just take you back to my parents' house," he said as his mouth covered mine.

I wanted to ask if he was serious, but the first touch of his lips and the slide of his tongue over my bottom lip made all else fade away. Going up onto my tiptoes, I grabbed his biceps and leaned into him, hungry for the taste, the connection, that I only ever wanted from him.

His hands grabbed my waist, and my feet left the ground. We began moving, but didn't go far. He lowered us to the sofa until he was sitting and I was straddling his lap. Not once breaking the kiss.

"You sleep in too many fucking clothes," he murmured against my lips.

My pajamas consisted of a pair of flannel pants and a tank top. His hands slid down my waist, and when he began to pull up the hem of my shirt, I lifted my arms, only releasing his mouth long enough for him to take the offending item off and toss it to the floor.

I moaned into his kiss as his hands covered my bare breasts, squeezing. The bulge in his pants pressed against my core, and I began to rock on it. Kash lifted his hips, making the contact more intense. When I cried out, I was suddenly off his lap, as he picked me up and stood me on the floor in front of him. The wild gleam in his eyes made me tremble as he took the waistline of my pants and jerked them down, along with my panties, leaving me completely bare. He only took a moment to let his eyes drift over my body, then went to the button on his jeans and began to unfasten them before shoving them off and kicking them aside.

The heat in his gaze flared when his eyes left my body to stare up into my eyes again. He held out a hand to me, and I slid mine into his.

As he brought me back to his lap, I went back to the position I'd been in before. My breathing quickened, along with my heart rate.

"I'm clean. I've been tested recently. There's been no one since," he said in a husky voice.

My breathing hitched when I realized what he was saying. He wanted to take me bare. With no barrier. We had done that before ... but back then, I'd been on birth control. He'd gotten it for me so that we could have sex without a condom.

"I-I'm not taking birth control," I admitted. "I don't, uh ... I haven't needed it." Because other than him taking me against the tree, I'd not had sex since him.

His eyes darkened. "That shouldn't make me as fucking happy as it does," he said as he ran his fingers through my hair. "I want you like this. Nothing between us. I'm not going anywhere. You can't get rid of me. So, the consequences don't scare me. They might just excite me, if I'm honest." He smirked then. "I'd have you locked to me that way."

A laugh bubbled out of me. The thought of being locked to Kash wasn't a threat. More like a dream. One I prayed I never woke up from. I'd spent the past four years going through the motions of living. Fighting to survive, but I'd been void of any happiness. There was no joy. My soul had been lost.

He brought it all back to me.

"Okay," I replied, sounding breathless.

His hands tightened their grip on my upper thighs. "Don't look so damn happy about it," he warned. "I'll end up fucking you so goddamn much that you're walking around with my cum leaking out of your sweet little pussy all the time."

The tremor that ran through me at his words was my only response. Kash's hands moved to my waist, and he positioned me over his thick, long erection. I dropped my gaze to watch as I took him. Sinking down while he stretched me. The slight pain from his size and my lack of action only added to the pleasure.

"Fuuuck," he hissed, and my head snapped up to see he was watching it too. Our joining.

When I was completely full, his head fell back, and he closed his eyes. The veins on his neck stood out, and he reminded me of a powerful god. I waited, not moving until he lifted his head and stared into my eyes.

He said nothing as he took my waist and began to pull me up slightly and then lower me back down. We did this several times before the building tingle became more frantic, and I took over, grabbing his shoulders, needing more. As I sped up the action, he began to thrust into me, making the sensation even more incredible. His eyes went down to my breasts, and he reached up to pinch one of my nipples, rolling it between his thumb and forefinger.

"That's it; ride me, little Songbird. Let me watch these pretty titties bounce while you take my cock," he groaned.

"Oh," I whimpered.

His dirty words heightened my pleasure. I loved his voice, but when it was like this, it was the sexiest sound in the world. My body began to quake. A cry of frustration tore from me as he picked me up and moved me from him. My back hit the sofa, and his palms pressed against my inner thighs, spreading me open. Then he was there over me, entering me hard, fast, verging on painful.

"Fuck!" he shouted as he started slamming into me, his body glistening with sweat, his eyes savage as they devoured me. "My cunt! My fucking tight cunt! Tell me, Songbird," he urged. "Tell me it's mine."

I nodded. "It's yours."

It always had been. All of me had been his since the moment he'd spoken to me. Even before he wanted me, I'd only wanted him.

His eyes flared again, and the crest I was climbing toward exploded. I screamed his name, clawing at his shoulders and chest as wave after wave crashed over me.

Kash let out a roar, and the first pulse of his release filled me so deeply that I felt it. The heat pouring into me. He shuddered.

"Cressida." My name fell from his lips on a hoarse cry. "Fuck, baby, that's it. Take all of it." He continued to pump into me.

My body jerked as another orgasm hit me. Kash pulled me into his arms and held me. We stayed like that while our erratic breathing slowed. I felt no regret. There was no fear. Instead, I lay there, feeling complete. Home. Exactly where I belonged.

TWENTY-SIX
KASH

Lifting myself off her, I slid free of her tight hole and held myself up with one hand, gripping the back of the sofa, while the other pushed her leg out so that her thighs were spread for me. I had to see it. The animal inside of me needed to see it. My seed dripping out of her sweet cunt. No, MY sweet cunt. She was mine. I'd claimed her years ago, possibly at first sight. That was never changing.

"What are you doing?" she asked, her voice just above a whisper.

"Watching my cum leak out of that perfect pink pussy," I replied with a quick grin before returning my attention back to between her legs.

She laughed. "Kash."

My name on her lips was my favorite sound. She tried to close her legs, and I shook my head, tsking at her as I continued to keep them like they were.

"I'm just gonna play with it a little. Rub it all over the inside of your thighs. Mark what's mine."

Her body trembled, and my eyes shot back up to hers as my cock began to twitch and come back to life.

"You want more?"

She blushed. "Already?"

I nodded.

"You can do that?"

I nodded again. "Seems my cock is as obsessed as I am."

A small, trickling laugh came from her, and my chest felt so damn full that it might explode. This was real. I was getting to have her. No more lies, misunderstandings, no more torture. I was home. I was with her.

"This isn't the Christmas I was expecting," she said. "I think I believe in Santa Claus again."

I leaned down over her, sliding my hands between her legs so I could play with her soaked pussy. "It's been one hell of a Christmas," I agreed. "And Santa Claus is fucking real."

She let out a soft moan. "Kash, I love you."

I paused and stared down at her. "You're my soul, my obsession, and my home," I told her.

Tears glistened in her eyes as she looked up at me. She was every wish I'd ever made. The light in the darkness that I'd thought I'd always walk in, and the thought of losing her again was something I couldn't live through. I wasn't a kid anymore. I was a man. One who knew who owned him and accepted it. Fucking reveled in it. Without her, I was nothing. I was void.

I hung my head and sighed heavily. The weight of not just the fear I felt over my mother's illness, but the sudden understanding of what my father was going through at facing a future without her in it.

"Kash ..." The worry in Cressida's voice as her hand touched my cheek comforted me in a way nothing else could since I'd been told about Mom.

157

I lifted my head again, meeting her concerned gaze. "Mom," I managed to get her name out without cracking. This wasn't something I wanted to talk about tonight. I had planned on it just being us. But right now, I needed her in another way. A way I'd never needed or wanted anyone else. "Mom is sick."

Cressida tensed beneath me. Her eyes widening. "How sick?" she whispered.

"Bad," I admitted. "I'll explain it later, but right now, I need you again. You're the only thing that eases the pain."

She nodded and leaned up to cover my mouth with hers. "When you're ready to talk, I'm here. I'll always be here." Her words, although soft, sounded fierce.

I buried my face in the crook of her neck and inhaled as the first real tears filled my eyes since I'd been told about my mom's diagnosis.

I didn't know what the next year would bring. My mom's future hung in the balance. But she had given me the one person back that I needed to survive it. Somehow, she had figured out who it was I needed and worked her magic.

There would only ever be two women in my life that were a part of me. The one who had raised me, loved me, and watched over me. And the one who owned my soul.

For now, I had them both, and I would cherish every moment.

Coming January 2026

UP TO NO GOOD – The rest of the Savelle family story unfolds when Forge gets his story.

ABOUT ABBI

Abbi Glines is a #1 New York Times, USA Today, Wall Street Journal, and International bestselling author of the Rosemary Beach, Sea Breeze, Smoke Series, Vincent Boys, Boys South of the Mason Dixon, and The Field Party Series. She is also author to the Sweet Trilogy and the Black Souls Trilogy. She believes in ghosts and has a habit of asking people if their house is haunted before she goes in it. Her house was built in 1820 and she finally has her own haunted house but they're friendly spirits. She drinks afternoon tea because she wants to be British but alas she was born in Alabama although she now lives in New England (which makes her feel a little closer to the British). When asked how many books she has written she has to stop and count on her fingers and even then she still forgets a few. When she's not locked away writing, she is entertaining her first grade daughter, she is reading (if everyone in her house including the ghosts will leave her alone long enough), shopping online (major Amazon Prime addiction), and planning her next Disney World vacation (and now that her oldest daughter Annabelle works at Disney she has an excuse to frequent it often).

You can connect with Abbi online in several different ways. She uses social media to procrastinate.

Facebook: AbbiGlinesAuthor
Twitter: abbiglines
Instagram: abbiglines
Snapchat: abbiglines
TikTok: abbiglines

Printed in Dunstable, United Kingdom

77190384R00112